In Cold Chamomile

Also available by Joy Avon

Sweet Tea and Secrets

In Peppermint Peril

In Cold Chamomile

A TEA AND A READ MYSTERY

Joy Avon

NEW YORK

This is a work of fiction. All of the names, characters, organizations, places, and events portrayed in this novel are either products of the author's imagination or are used fictitiously. Any resemblance to real or actual events, locales, or persons, living or dead, is entirely coincidental.

Published in the United States by Crooked Lane Books, an imprint of The Quick Brown Fox & Company LLC.

Crooked Lane Books and its logo are trademarks of The Quick Brown Fox & Company LLC.

Library of Congress Catalog-in-Publication data available upon request.

ISBN (hardcover): 978-1-64385-288-1
ISBN (ebook): 978-1-64385-309-3

Cover illustration by Brandon Dorman
Book design by Jennifer Canzone

Printed in the United States.

www.crookedlanebooks.com

Crooked Lane Books
34 West 27th St., 10th Floor
New York, NY 10001

First Edition: February 2020

10 9 8 7 6 5 4 3 2 1

Chapter One

"One red heart for the day of love."

Callie Aspen attached the red heart badge with her name to the lapel of her jacket and checked in the car's rear-view mirror that it was in the right spot. Then she threw a regretful look at the empty passenger seat where her Boston terrier Daisy normally sat, strapped in her basket. But the Valentine's event today would pull in so many visitors that it would make the quiet little dog uncomfortable, and Callie had decided to leave her at Book Tea, where the regular helpers would look after her.

She got out of the car and took a moment to soak up the sunshine slanting across her face. It shone down from a pale blue winter sky, streaked with errant clouds, and turned the frost left on Haywood Hall's lawn into little twinkles, as if someone had strewn diamonds across it. The house itself looked cozy, with smoke coming from the many chimneys, indicating the hearths were well fed, and welcome warmth would wrap itself around Callie as soon as she stepped inside.

But it wasn't just warmth waiting for her behind the broad front door, which was the exact reason she stood a little while longer to breathe the crisp air and listen for the sound of birds in the nearby trees. It was so wonderfully quiet. And inside it would be hectic, full of the bustle of furniture being moved around, people shouting orders at one another, panicky last-minute discussions about the best place for a buffet table or about a notebook with important directions that had been mislaid. And as one of the organizers, most queries would be directed to her, demanding an instant solution.

Their Valentine's event consisted of six main themes, which had seemed manageable when Callie and her great-aunt Iphy had thought it up, but as it had started to unfold, more and more people had gotten involved, and at last count they had over a hundred. Everybody was anxious that his or her part in it would go off without a hitch, and they all called Callie at every hour of the day with new ideas or old concerns. The leader of the baroque orchestra that would perform in the old ballroom had proven to be especially difficult, having at first praised Haywood Hall's acoustics, then deemed them disastrous for his group's performance. His violinist had complained about a draft on her neck, and the singer who was supposed to perform with them hadn't even shown up for rehearsals. There was no shortage of big egos around, and Callie could feel a headache forming just thinking of dealing with all of these people.

She took a deep breath and walked up to the front door, taking a moment to touch the railing along the steps, which was also adorned with a layer of frost. It felt cold under her fingertips but melted instantly, betraying that the heart of winter was past, and spring was on its way.

Callie found the front door ajar and pushed it open, ready to face the attack of voices and noises, hunt for the first notes of discord and the need for her to step in and soothe.

But to her surprise, music filled the air, and several people stood listening to it, their clipboards clutched under their arms. A flute played a haunting solo, and then the entire orchestra joined in, sending waves of beguiling music through the house.

Callie closed her eyes and hummed along, thinking it would indeed be easy to fall in love with this wonderful performance.

"Callie! There you are, at last. You're at least five minutes late."

Callie cringed and snapped her eyes open to face a frail elderly lady sailing down on her with indignation in her every step. Gray curls peeked out from under a snug felt hat adorned with a diamond hatpin. The curls trembled on her narrow shoulders as she marched up and put her hands on her hips. "I called you several times."

"I'm sorry, Mrs. Forrester. I was driving and couldn't answer the phone."

Mrs. Forrester gave her a long hard look, as if she saw right through that thin excuse. She had been a teacher all of her life and still treated people like they were squirming kids who hadn't done their homework. Iphy had warned Callie in advance that including a secondhand book market would mean bringing in Mrs. Forrester, but to be honest, Callie had wondered how bad that could be. They needed books to be a part of the event, first because Haywood Hall had an amazing library that was being catalogued as part of the house's conservation program; second because her great-aunt's business, Book Tea, was all about the combination of books and tea; and third because if there was an object in the world you could easily fall in love with, it had to be books. Callie could remember so many lazy afternoons as a girl lying in the grass reading. Or late at night in bed, reading until she fell asleep with the book beside her. That was the life.

As Haywood Hall's book collection was rather precious, they had decided that a secondhand book market would be an amazing complement, and the library and adjacent study were now divided into several areas for bookworms: a swap corner, where you could trade your own book for another, a blind date corner where you could buy a mystery book wrapped up in colorful paper, and a "find out the value" corner where old books could be offered for an appraisal by an expert in old books and antiques.

The expert had been brought in by Mrs. Forrester, who knew him from another occasion, and she had also supplied most of the books for the swapping as she was a volunteer at the local library and had convinced them to donate to the event part of what they were getting rid of from the collection. Without her input and persuasiveness, the book-themed part of the event would have been much smaller. Callie should be very grateful to Mrs. Forrester, she knew, and honestly she was, but she did wish deep down that the woman's helpfulness would be wrapped up in more kindness. She was so prompt and abrupt and to the point all of the time that it felt rather unpleasant to have to deal with her.

"What could be so urgent?" Callie asked Mrs. Forrester, who widened her eyes as if she was appalled at the question.

Mrs. Forrester stretched out her arm so that her silver watch became visible on her slender wrist, and checked the time ostentatiously. "The Valentine's event is scheduled to begin in three hours, and you ask me what could be so urgent?"

She raised both her hands and waved them in a dramatic fashion. "All the things that are not done yet, not provided for."

Her emphasis stoked Callie's nerves, and she asked, "What is not arranged for? I thought we had the whole thing worked out."

Mrs. Forrester gave her a scorching look. "For instance, the expert who is to evaluate the value of the books people bring in, Mr. King "—she spoke the name with a sort of hushed awe—"who will bring him coffee?"

Callie blinked. "I thought one of you would have a thermos stashed somewhere and could pour him a cup if he wants some."

"He is not a local you can fob off with a plastic cup full of powdered coffee. He is an expert whose time is extremely valuable. He appraises books on television! He could be anywhere this afternoon, but I persuaded him to come *here*, for free, as this is a charitable event. That doesn't mean, however, that we can treat him like his services aren't worth anything."

"Of course not," Callie said, rather shocked that her practical solution was being viewed in this manner. "I only thought that—"

"You own a tearoom," Mrs. Forrester said, stabbing at Callie with a French-manicured fingernail. "You are supposed to serve people the best mocha and the most exquisite treats."

"We are," Callie said, straightening under the censure. "The drawing room is our Valentine's salon, where we serve—"

"He can't leave his table. You will have to come and serve him."

For a moment Callie saw a scene where she entered the room dressed in a black gown with a little white apron, like you saw in old-timey TV shows, and made a curtsey as she put the coffee down for his lordship, the book evaluator, asking him in a deferential tone if he needed anything else.

But she didn't dare laugh at the idea, as Mrs. Forrester seemed to be completely in earnest.

"I will mention it to Iphy," Callie said demurely. "Anything else?"

Mrs. Forrester sighed and let her gaze wander the hallway. "I think it could all have been done more professionally. Those signs . . ." She stared hard at a nearby cardboard placard, white with red lettering, reading "Fall in Love with Books," with an arrow pointing up the stairs. Hearts of all sizes in bright red and pink danced around the letters. Callie agreed that it might be a bit much, but after all, this was a Valentine's event, and people did expect to see some sort of heart theme, she supposed.

"It should have been black with golden lettering," Mrs. Forrester declared. "A little more class and style, as befits these elegant surroundings. So much history within these walls, and you fill the place with heart-shaped balloons." She stared in disgust at the helium-filled balloons that floated gently above the stairs' railing.

Callie didn't know quite what to say to that, and she was glad that at that moment she caught movement out of the corner of her eye and saw Iphy coming in with Peggy and two other Book Tea helpers, carrying coolers and cartons full of supplies.

Breathing a sigh of relief, Callie excused herself to Mrs. Forrester and rushed to help Iphy navigate the enormous box she was carrying. Callie knew it held part of the cake for the event, and her heart beat nervously at the idea that the heart-shaped macarons would come off or the delicate sugar work crowning it would somehow be damaged. People didn't appreciate just the sweet taste of Iphy's creations but also her decorative imagination, and often took photos of her treats that they then shared online, bringing new visitors to Book Tea and new reservations for bookish tea parties.

As they put the box down on the table in the drawing room, Peggy said to Callie, "Was Mrs. Forrester throwing a fit again?"

She whipped back a lock of her blonde hair. When Callie had first gotten to know her, Peggy had just been to the hairdresser's for a perm, but these days her hair was straight, pulled back from her face into a ponytail. It made her look younger, carefree, almost like a student again. She was also wearing a new dress today, with high heels, and Callie wondered if she was hoping to run into anyone particular at this Valentine's event.

"Mrs. Forrester isn't that bad once you learn to see past the obvious," Iphy said gently while placing muffins with red frosting and tiny fondant teddy bears on plates. Her two helpers were setting up the coffee machine and stacking cups, mugs, and glasses.

No plastic cups here, Callie thought with a sour look, recalling Mrs. Forrester's critique. But she supposed it was too late to appease the irate volunteer now.

"Oh, there's Quinn," Iphy exclaimed, pointing at the door. Callie didn't look in that direction first, but at Peggy, who was suddenly completely engrossed in rearranging the ginger letter cookies people could use to spell names or words, laying out a message of love for someone with them at the event. Peggy's cheeks were suspiciously red, but then it was rather hot in the room, especially if you had just come in from the chill outside.

Quinn seemed to be gesturing to them, so Callie headed over. Quinn was wearing a neat white shirt with a tie and jeans, and he had his border collie, Biscuit, by his side. Callie saw the dog was also wearing a red bow tie attached to his collar. She had to smile, as the bow tie symbolized what a true gentleman the dog had become in the past few months.

Quinn had adopted Biscuit the previous summer, after his elderly owners had decided he was too much for them at their age and wanted to return him to the rescue where they had found him. But Callie had believed Biscuit's trust in people might be damaged if he was returned to the rescue again, and had arranged for Quinn to take care of him for a while. The two of them soon bonded and were inseparable. The idea of him ever going back to the rescue was long forgotten, and Biscuit was a welcome face in his new hometown, with people stopping Quinn in the street to pat Biscuit or ask if Quinn could show them something new the dog had learned.

These days Biscuit was perfectly well behaved and even an example to other dogs Quinn worked with at the local shelter.

"One of the heaters in the stables isn't working," Quinn explained to Callie. "The temperatures are rather chilly for the animals to be there all afternoon. Do you have a toolbox around so I can see if I can fix it?"

"Sure, in the conservatory closet, I think. Follow me." Callie was glad Quinn had proven to be handy, doing repairs on the cottage she had rented when she had come to live in Heart's Harbor. Not only had he fixed what was broken, but he had also painted and wallpapered, turning the rather sparse little place into a brand-new home for her.

Smiling at the recollection, she led the way through the hallway, past the sign reading "Fall in Love with Plants," down a corridor and into the conservatory, which had once been the domain of Haywood Hall's gardener, Mr. Leadenby.

Callie felt a stab of sadness as she recalled his sudden death and the events it had put into motion. It was difficult still to think about his death, but they had all banded together to solve the murder and save the house. That was something that would have meant the world to Leadenby. Yes, a day like today, with people flocking in to admire his orchids on display and swap plants and seeds, would have been something after his own heart.

Biscuit had his head up at the many strange scents assaulting his sensitive nose, and he turned this way and that to look at the gardening enthusiasts who were setting up shop.

Callie greeted a few people as she made her way to the large wooden closets against the far wall and opened a door to search inside. The metal toolbox should be on one of the shelves. She recalled it was bright blue.

Yes, there it was. She breathed an inaudible sigh of relief that she had found it in a single try and didn't have to hunt for it elsewhere in the large house. Mrs. Forrester's insistence that there was too little time to get everything done before the event had started to make her jumpy.

"There you are." She pulled the toolbox out of the closet and handed it to Quinn. It was quite heavy, but he carried it in one hand. "I hope you can fix it. I don't think we can bring in another heater on such short notice."

"I'll have a look, and if I can't fix it, I'll call around and see if anyone can help out." Quinn smiled at her. His quiet confidence that locals would help him was a testimony to how well he had integrated into his new hometown. Callie knew he had only planned to spend a few weeks in Heart's Harbor that summer, but work offers had kept him around, and these days she believed Quinn was about as much a resident as the rest of them. His volunteer work at the shelter and the meal project for lonely elderly citizens had enabled him to meet lots of new people in a short period of time, and she knew some of the ladies considered him to be almost like a grandson.

Callie smiled as she watched him walk out the conservatory door that led into the garden, to round the house to the stables, where the animal portion of their event would be. Quinn had made the suggestion himself that they should have a "Fall in Love with Dogs" event, where people could meet some of the shelter's dogs currently looking for new homes and get information on how to adopt them. "It's not meant as a sentimental moment where people are tricked into getting a pet because they feel sorry for the poor doggy," he had said with conviction. "I want people to understand what they're getting into. I don't want to hand out our charges and then get them back within a few days because it doesn't turn out the way the new owners expected."

They had agreed that the event would focus not just on finding the eligible dogs a new home but also on engaging people with the shelter, perhaps getting some new volunteers or donations. "A win–win," Iphy had called it with a smile.

Callie rolled back her tight shoulders and looked around her, sniffing the scents of the tropical plants. The warm damp air folded itself around her, and she longed to linger a bit with people who were not rushing or scolding one another, but rather quietly putting things in place and chattering about how much they looked forward to the afternoon's visitors. Someone passed around lemonade in plastic cups, and Callie noted, with a wry thought of Mrs. Forrester's demands, that here nobody seemed to feel above drinking from a plastic cup.

Still, the reminder of the honored expert with television credentials who was about to arrive at the Hall sent her darting back into the hallway, determined to treat the man with all due respect. After all, he was offering his time for free. Callie had gotten the impression from a quick look at his website that he had become a celebrity overnight, after a TV appearance, around Christmas of the previous year, on a show where people bring in their flea-market and garage-sale treasures to see if they happened to be worth a fortune.

In any case, Mrs. Forrester had insisted on advertising their event in the local paper, with the man's name and photograph prominently on display, and several regional papers had also run it, claiming a "TV star" was visiting Heart's Harbor. It was good promotion for the event, and Callie kept her fingers crossed that the star wouldn't have an attitude that turned people off.

Just as she was about to turn into the drawing room again, a tall, gray-haired man came through the front door. He walked very upright and looked about him with keen brown eyes. There was a certain joie de vivre about him, an energy that immediately captured attention. He took in the decorations, the heart-shaped balloons, the signs with the red lettering that Mrs. Forrester had deemed inferior, and smiled. The warmth of that smile made his features even more attractive, and Callie concluded with a grin that in his younger years he had probably been a regular heartbreaker. Why, even now ladies were turning their heads and poking one another with their elbows.

Callie stepped forward and said, "Good afternoon, may I help you? You're here for the event?"

"Yes, I'm Sean Strong. The baritone."

Callie hesitated a moment as her mind conjured up another name for the singer, but with so many participants, she could have mixed up a name or two. She reached out her hand. "Oh yes, you're going to perform with the orchestra. How nice to meet you at last."

Recalling her earlier judgment about the presumed ego of the absent soloist, her cheeks flushed a little as she shook his hand.

He smiled widely. "I'm so sorry I couldn't be here sooner. I've just ended a string of performances in Vienna and only flew in this morning."

Callie's jaw sagged. "You just stepped off a plane from Europe?"

"Yes. Normally I would have stayed in Vienna for a few more days, but as I was asked to come here . . ." He made a gesture with both hands. "I couldn't say no. Such a good cause, a beautiful old house."

Callie's face heated even more as she realized how this kind man had made room in his busy schedule to perform with them, and she had judged him for not being there earlier to rehearse. He had flown in especially for them!

What could she do to make him feel welcome, appreciated?

"I'm delighted you'll be singing here this afternoon," she said quickly. "Can I get you anything to eat or drink? Do you want to rest up?" Her mind raced to decide which room upstairs could be allotted to him for the moment. She recollected vaguely that there had been a decision that Mr. King, the antiques appraiser, would also need a room to retreat to if he wanted, and she wasn't sure what room had been chosen for him. She could hardly double-book.

"Actually," he said quietly, "I would very much like to see the room where we will be performing and meet the director of the orchestra so we can talk through the performance."

He leaned over to her. "I'm a perfectionist, and I can't rest until I know I can perform under the right conditions to offer my audience the best possible experience."

"Of course." Callie swallowed a moment, hoping the space would be to his liking. Her heart beat fast as she led him to the ballroom door. The orchestra had stopped playing, and the director stood talking to one of the members while others were either checking their instruments or walking about a bit to stretch their legs.

The director saw Callie and Mr. Strong and waved. "Ah, Sean! Glad you could make it."

It sounded a bit cynical, and Callie rushed over to explain that Mr. Strong had just flown in from Europe and was happy to have some time to rehearse before the actual performance. "We're so pleased he made the time to be here," she ended, with a pleading expression at the director.

The director sighed but welcomed Strong with a handshake and an introduction to the other members. Callie didn't miss the excited looks of the ladies among the company. Strong didn't seem to notice; he was looking at the music on the stand and then studying the height of the room as if deducing something about the sound when he would start to sing. He flexed his shoulders as he stood and accepted a glass of water from a lady who got envious looks from the others. *This seems to be going down well. All right, what next?* Callie turned away and wanted to leave the room. At the door was Iphy, who seemed to need her for something. Her great-aunt's expression was eager as always but changed completely when she glanced past Callie. All color drained from her face, and she stared as if she had seen something horrible.

Callie looked back at the orchestra and then to Iphy to determine what on earth could be so upsetting. Her great-aunt had raised a hand to her mouth and then turned around in a jerk and rushed off.

Callie ran after her. "Iphy!" She overtook her and rested a hand on her shoulder. "Is something wrong? It looks like you've had a shock."

Iphy kept on walking, through the corridor into the kitchen, where nothing was stirring. She stood at the sink and leaned her hands on the edge. She took a deep breath, steadying herself.

"Are you okay?" Callie urged. "Do you want a glass of water? Yes, you have to sit down." She took her great-aunt by the arm, directed her to a chair, and pushed her into it. Then she got a glass out of the cupboard and filled it with water at the tap. The water was cold against the glass, and Callie shivered a moment as she handed it to Iphy. The sudden turn in her great-aunt's mood had unsettled her, and she wanted to know what was up. But Iphy didn't seem able to explain anything. She simply stared ahead without blinking.

"There you go." Callie held out the glass. Iphy accepted it with a mechanical gesture but didn't seem to understand she had to raise it to her lips and take a sip.

"I can't believe it," she whispered. "It can't be true. He can't be here." She suddenly made eye contact with Callie. "What is he doing here?"

Callie didn't follow. "Who do you mean?"

"Sean." The name came out like a gasp.

"Oh, the baritone. He's here to sing."

"No, he's not our baritone. I know who was coming. I would have known it was him as soon as I saw his name on the program. Our baritone is someone else. Why isn't he here? Why did Sean come in his stead?"

Callie frowned. So, her first impression that the name Sean Strong didn't match the name of the expected performer had been correct.

She reached into her jacket pocket and produced the program she had put together weeks before. She was carrying it in case anyone had questions about it, but hadn't looked at it yet that day.

She opened it and ran her eyes over all the entries. There it was. Cycle of Liebeslieder, or love songs, by various German composers, performed by . . .

Simon Teak.

She blinked, but it was really there.

She looked up at Iphy. "You're right. Our baritone listed here is Simon Teak. The man who just walked in is—"

"Sean Strong." Iphy leaned back against the chair, clutching her glass. "I can't believe it. Why would he show his face here again?"

"He's been here before? You know him?"

Iphy seemed to focus on Callie for the very first time. She startled upright, almost spilling the water across her neat dress. "It's not important, really. What did he say for why he was here?"

"He didn't say anything. Just that he had flown in from Europe this morning. He's been performing in Vienna, and now he's here, because it was for a good cause and all, and in a beautiful venue. I was sure he was our baritone. Why would he pop up here if he didn't have to? It can't be cheap to fly from Vienna. And where is Simon Teak?"

Iphy had sagged again and was sitting with her head down, her hands tight around the water glass.

"I'll go ask him," Callie said and rushed off with the program in her hand. She found Strong in a deep discussion with the lead violinist of the orchestra. She tapped his arm. "Excuse me a moment, but something is unclear. Our agreement was with the baritone Simon Teak, but you just introduced yourself to me as Sean Strong."

"Oh, didn't I mention that?" He flashed his heartthrob smile again. "Simon is ill. Nothing serious, just a little throat infection, but it does affect his voice. He asked me to take his place. For the good cause and all that. I agreed to it. I have a thing for old houses." He eyed her with a twinkle in his brown eyes. "Is there a problem?"

Callie shook her head. "No, not at all—very kind of you to take Mr. Teak's place. I wish him a speedy recovery."

"I'll tell him when I talk to him." Strong nodded at her and returned his attention to the violinist, who had waited impatiently with his sheet music in hand.

Callie slowly retraced her steps to the kitchen. It was a coincidence. A man falling ill, another taking his place. Inadvertently returning to a place he had apparently been before. But if it was such a long time ago, would he even remember?

Iphy obviously did.

Callie swallowed when she realized she had to tell her great-aunt it was indeed Sean Strong taking the place of the man they had asked to come.

Iphy was still sitting there, frozen in shock. She had not touched her water.

Callie said, "It's all clear now." She tried to sound light and casual. "The man we asked to come turns out to be ill with a throat infection. Mr. Strong kindly offered to take his place."

"Offered? When he knew he was coming here?" Iphy sat motionless, a deep frown over her eyes, as if she was trying to work out something she couldn't quite get a handle on.

Callie closed in on her and leaned over. "Do you know him?"

Iphy looked up. She blinked as if suddenly aware of Callie's presence and the fact that she wanted to know things.

"He performed here before. It didn't turn out . . . Well, it wasn't his fault, I suppose."

Iphy shook her head with an impatient insistence and rose to her feet. She put the glass of water on the table with a thud that suggested her usual determination was coming back to her. "It's just silly of me. I hadn't expected to ever see him again."

"He performed here? In Heart's Harbor? Years ago?"

"A lifetime ago." Iphy's voice was soft, her eyes staring as if into a distant past. "He wasn't well known then. Not a world traveler like he is now." She looked at Callie, her keen brisk self again. "Well, I suppose it's just a coincidence then. People do fall ill at the most inconvenient moments."

She hesitated a few seconds, fidgeting with her hands. "I would appreciate it if you do not mention to him that you know he was here before. I will certainly act like I don't remember."

"But . . ." Callie searched for the right words.

"I just said it didn't turn out well at the time. Bringing it up would just be painful. And Mr. Strong is doing us a favor by taking the sick baritone's place. We should treat him with respect."

Callie wondered whether Iphy meant to imply that there had been some scandal surrounding Mr. Strong's previous performance in Heart's Harbor and that it was better for everyone involved to act as if said performance had never happened. Callie agreed that making their guest uncomfortable should be the last thing they wanted. So she nodded. "Okay. I really don't know him at all, so it won't be hard."

"I'll just stay out of his way." Iphy walked to the door. "I won't come to the performance."

"But you said you wanted to hear it. That you loved these Liebeslieder."

"It doesn't matter much. Hopefully, it will be so crowded at our tea event I won't be able to leave anyway." Iphy smiled at her, a wan forced smile. "It will be all right. Just act like you have no idea, Callie." Then she left the kitchen in a rush.

Chapter Two

"There are more lemon macarons in the trunk of my car," Peggy said to Callie. Her cheeks were red from the heat in the room and from rushing around to serve everyone. She carried a tray with mint teas and cappuccinos for a nearby table.

Callie said, "I'll go get them. Give me the key."

Balancing the tray against her hip, Peggy extracted the car key from her pocket and handed it to Callie, who rushed off with it. In the hallway she almost bumped into Mr. Bates. The pet portrait painter, who had done a stunning portrait of Daisy, beamed at her. "What an excellent event. Personally I have no appreciation for Valentine's Day at all—this whole commercial thing with having to buy presents and all—but you gave it a fun twist. I was just up in the library." He pulled a book out from under his arm. "I handed in my leather-bound edition of *War and Peace*, which I have read countless times, and got this."

He showed her a big book with reproductions of oil paintings. "I can leaf through this for hours. I'm already looking forward to it. Now, for a cup of hot chocolate before the concert begins. An excellent event!" Without waiting for a response, he bustled away into the drawing room.

With a grin on her face, Callie headed outside and found Peggy's car, tucked in between two other cars. She opened the trunk and dove halfway in, reaching for the plastic carrier box full of yellow macarons. There was also one with purple macarons, maybe blueberry flavored, and she decided to take that one in as well. Just as she pulled it toward her, she heard female voices.

One said, "I don't know if we should really do this."

The other said, "Of course we should. We decided this weeks ago. Don't be such a spoilsport."

A short silence, as if the other woman was considering what to say in return, and then voice two, determined and a bit spiteful, said once more, "You want him to get his just desserts as much as I do. So let's get on with it."

Callie extracted the box from the trunk and, turning her head in the direction of the voices, saw two women in woolen coats and big scarves, each carrying a large canvas bag. She didn't know who they were or even what age they might be, as she could just see their backs, moving away from her at a brisk pace. But the snippets of their conversation had seemed a bit odd.

Just desserts? For whom?

Callie shook her head as she closed the trunk and made sure it was locked. She tended to puzzle over a remark made, tried to place it in context even if she knew very little, simply because she loved to deduce, but this was silly. She had no idea what it had all been about and whether she had even heard it correctly, what with her head stuck in the trunk.

The wind breathed through the thin fabric of her dress, and shivering, she hurried back to the house with the extra macarons. Back inside, in the bustle of tea drinkers in the drawing room, she was glad to see Iphy serving and talking and laughing like her usual self. The shock of finding Sean Strong at Haywood Hall seemed to have worn off. Callie's own discomfort had evaporated with the reassurance her great-aunt was well, and she passed both boxes of macarons to a Book Tea helper and retreated to see how things were going in the other themed areas. She first ventured out to the conservatory, passing a lady carrying a huge blossoming pink orchid, just remarking that she had never had one with so many blooms yet. For a moment Callie thought the woman was speaking to herself, until she detected the earpiece, suggesting she was on the phone with someone.

In the conservatory, seed packets were changing hands by auction. Lively bidding was going on, reaching prices that probably more represented people's desire to sponsor Haywood Hall than to own these particular seeds for their gardens or balconies. Callie saw some nice geraniums that she could put in hanging baskets at her cottage once it was a little warmer, and the seller offered to drop by later in the year and bring the geraniums to her. "White and pink, or red—you tell me closer to the time." He passed her a card with contact information, and she slipped it into her pocket.

Then Callie went upstairs to the library, where, in the swap corner, two women were each holding on to the same book, each claiming she had picked it up first. "I handed in my copy of *Great Expectations* for it. Now I want it!" said one.

"But I saw it first, and I was already holding it when you tried to wrench it from my hands," the other countered. Mrs. Forrester, turning her head this way and that, tried in vain to appease them and get one of them to let the other have it.

Callie acted like she didn't notice the discord, and passed by to have a look at the expert evaluating the offered goods. Mr. King was a tall man with dark hair—dyed, Callie believed—and a pair of horn-rimmed glasses. A look of perpetual disapproval seemed glued to his long, thin face as he studied the leather spine of a book on the table before him. His lean fingers moved over it, assessing its condition, and then he shook his head with the sad certainty of an undertaker. "This is virtually worthless. I could give you twenty dollars for it, no more."

The elderly couple who had brought it in looked at each other. The woman fidgeted with the clasp of her purse, snapping it open and then shutting it again. Snap, snap, snap. "It comes from my mother's inheritance," she said in a thin voice.

Her husband retorted at once, "You have so many of her things. This is just gathering dust in the attic. Let's take the twenty dollars."

The woman didn't seem sure, but the expert had already pulled out money and handed it to the man, pulling the book toward him and handing it off to a young man who put it in a wooden crate that stood on the floor behind the expert's table. Callie saw it contained quite a lot of books already. She hoped the locals would at least be happy with the deals offered to them and wouldn't in hindsight regret having parted with something valuable.

She was just about to turn away again and continue her inspection of the event's themed areas, when she saw the two women from outside in the parking lot, now carrying their woolen coats over their arms. They still had their scarves wrapped around their necks, though, and one of them was ducking into hers as if she was still cold. They each had their canvas bags at the ready, and Callie concluded they contained books the women wanted to offer to Mr. King for assessment.

Perhaps one of the ladies had taken them from her husband's book collection at home and wasn't sure whether he would agree that they should part with them? And her friend thought it would be his just desserts if she did? Maybe because he was always busy with those books and ignored his wife?

Callie! You don't know anything about it. Cut it out.

Callie passed the women, noticing absentmindedly that one of them was probably ten years younger than the other. She looked a bit insecure, and her brown eyes were darting around the room as if looking for a way out. But the other woman, blonde with gray streaks and a very straight posture, ushered her forward.

Callie smiled at them and then exited, determined to go check on the stables and make sure that the heater Quinn had managed to fix wasn't broken again.

Or overheating and starting a fire. The idea that there were a lot of live animals there made her heart speed up.

But when she entered the stables at a trot, welcome warmth enveloped her, and the chatter of excited people, especially children, filled her ears. Several volunteers sat crouched beside dogs they were introducing to the public. A big black poodle didn't seem to like the attention and tried to hide behind the volunteer's back, but when a little boy approached and played peekaboo, looking at the poodle and then stepping back out of sight, the dog became curious and showed himself. Slowly his tail began to wag, and the little boy smiled broadly.

Callie's heart widened at the idea that here relationships might begin that would last for the dog's lifetime. Animals that were currently living behind bars would find a new home today. If only for that, their event would be a success.

"Callie." Quinn rested his hand on her shoulder. His expression was relaxed, but at the same time she noticed a certain tension in him, as if he was eager for something to happen. His smile wasn't quite at ease, and his eyes brushed past her and roamed the room.

"How are things going?" she asked. "Is the heater fixed for real?"

"It's doing great. I think it'll last through the event."

"Good. That was what I wanted to know, really." Callie glanced around her. "Oh, I see you've got help."

Jimmy and Tate, Peggy's boys, were sitting on the other side of the stables, each with a retriever puppy in his arms. Their mother was watching them from her place on a blanket, with three more puppies clambering across her outstretched body.

Quinn nodded in their direction. "The dog was found roaming, turned out of her home, maybe after the owners discovered she was expecting. She gave birth to five healthy puppies a few weeks ago. We're now hoping to find good homes for them all."

"Are you trying to persuade Peggy to take one of them?" Callie frowned. "She's away a lot for her work at Book Tea, and the boys are in school, so who would be able to take care of a small dog?"

Quinn shrugged. "Her situation might not always stay like that."

Callie wanted to ask what on earth he meant by that, but growling and barking drew her attention in a flash. Two dogs had jumped at each other, teeth bared, and the volunteers struggled to pull them away. A frightened little girl burst into tears, hiding against her mother, and some parents looked less than happy, moving away and whispering as if deciding to leave.

Quinn shook his head. "I told Jerry not to bring that black Lab. He isn't ready to be re-homed. Too many new things make him nervous, and then he snaps. But they just don't listen to me. 'This is a chance of a lifetime,' they said.

Yes, well, but if his behavior turns the potential new owners off all the dogs present—"

"I'm sure it won't be that bad," Callie reassured him. But inside she wondered. People were right to think twice about taking a dog into their homes; after all, these weren't toys, but live animals that needed a lot of caring for. And if a dog also seemed to have a problem, it became extra hard.

She patted Quinn's arm. "I'm sure you'll find a few dogs good homes today. Talk to people, find out what they're looking for. Ask them to stop by the shelter and see more of the dog there. No impulse decisions, but growing relations."

Quinn nodded. "I know. I'm trying." He rubbed his hands together, his posture tense, as if he was gearing up for something.

Callie wasn't sure what it was that was eating at him, but she didn't want to ask right now. Having greeted the volunteers and ensured the black Lab was calm again and wagging his tail, she left the stables to go back to the house.

The cold air nipped at her, and she broke into a trot. Someone came from the other direction, and they reached the door at the same time. It was Sean Strong, the baritone, and he held the door open for her with a smile. "After you, young lady. You should have put on a coat."

"Yes, probably. Thank you," Callie said as she stepped inside.

Strong, who wasn't wearing a coat himself, followed her and stood a moment, as if indecisive. Then he said, "Tell me, can one get decent coffee here?"

"More than decent," Callie assured him. "The catering is done by Book Tea, a very good tearoom from town. We have delicious coffee, tea, and treats." She added quickly, "If you want some." Perhaps with his performance coming, he didn't want to eat? She had no idea if it affected the voice.

"That sounds very inviting." He smiled at her. "Would you mind pointing me in the right direction?"

For a moment Callie recalled her great-aunt's shock when she had recognized Strong and claimed that he had been to Heart's Harbor before and it hadn't ended well. But that had been, to recall Iphy's words, "a lifetime ago," so why would it matter today?

Besides, she could hardly pretend not to *know* where the coffee was served, when she was herself part of the Book Tea team. She forced a smile. "Not at all. Through this door."

Callie led Sean Strong into the drawing room, where the scent of mocha coffee and walnut cake filled the air. People were standing in groups as all of the seats were already taken. Callie and Sean had to push their way through to get to the long table where Iphy was serving. She was just lifting a new chocolate cake from a container and putting it on a plate, to start cutting it up. White frosting on top outlined a great house, which might be interpreted as Haywood Hall but could also represent Mr. Rochester's abode from *Jane Eyre* or iconic Pemberley.

Callie moved aside to let Strong reach the table and place an order. She looked at his face. To her surprise, he stared at her great-aunt with a look of worry in his eyes. A slight frown, an uncertainty that didn't seem to fit his confident attitude. Did he also recall his previous visit to this small town and the unfortunate events that had taken place?

What could they have been?

Iphy looked up. "May I . . ." The words *help you* seemed to die on her tongue as she stared at Strong. He held her gaze with that quiet, slightly concerned look. Then he smiled and said, "Hello, Iphy."

Callie's jaw sagged when he said her great-aunt's first name. Iphy had only let on that Strong had performed in town, but not that he had known her personally. Or had she been on some organizing committee at the time? Still, if it was that long ago, why would Strong, who apparently traveled the world, recall her at all?

"Hello, Sean." Iphy's voice was soft and slightly unstable. She straightened up in an attempt, it seemed, to regain control of the situation. "I heard you were replacing Mr. Teak this afternoon. I hope he isn't too ill?"

"No, he'll be fine. Really. Just a little throat trouble after a head cold. You know how that is." Strong seemed at a loss for further things to say. He just stared at Iphy, who stared back.

Callie wished she had told Strong to go back to the ballroom, where she would bring him his coffee order. It would have been better to avoid this confrontation. Even if she had no idea what it was about, it was obviously painful to both parties.

"This young lady here tells me you have amazing coffee," Strong said at last in a forced cheerful tone that sounded insincere.

"That young lady," Iphy replied, taking up the light tone, "is my great-niece, Callie Aspen. She has come to live in Heart's Harbor to help me with the Book Tea."

He frowned again. "Help you? Are you not well?"

"I'm fine, but I'm not getting any younger. Neither of us is, I suppose."

Strong seemed to want to protest, but then he nodded. "I suppose." He sighed, and Callie noticed that Iphy cast a worried look over his features, then down his figure, as if to see if something might be wrong with him.

Strong said, "I'd like a coffee, please."

Iphy checked her watch. "Isn't it too close before the performance?"

"Will you come and listen?"

"I can't leave here."

"Callie can take your place, I'm sure." Strong flashed a smile at Callie. "Your great-aunt loves classical music. Especially by German composers."

"I don't have the time." Iphy sounded more insistent now, almost annoyed.

Callie looked from one to the other. It was clear something had passed between them when they had met before, but what could it be?

Iphy poured coffee for Strong and handed the cup to him. As their hands touched briefly, Callie saw a flash of sadness in her great-aunt's eyes. As if she was sorry for something. For Strong? Had he done something wrong in the past, ruining things for himself in Heart's Harbor? But why then had he returned? He didn't have to take

Teak's place, she supposed. A throat infection was a valid reason to cancel, and they would simply have had to tell the audience the orchestra would perform without a baritone.

She accompanied him back to the door. "Did Mr. Teak ask you specifically to take his place? I mean, you were in Vienna, after all—it wasn't nothing to fly out here."

Strong glanced at her, a quick, almost suspicious look. "It was the best solution. All for a good cause, right?" He toasted her with the cup. "This smells delicious. Thank you." And he walked off.

Callie noticed he hadn't asked *her* to come and listen to his performance. Just Iphy. How odd. Not that she felt passed over or anything, but it had seemed as if he attached special importance to Iphy being there.

Callie shook her head. She shouldn't be too curious about things that were none of her business. Just as she was standing there, she saw the two women who had spoken about "just desserts" come back down the stairs. The younger one was carrying a bag that seemed much emptier now. So they had sold off something to the antiques appraiser. They didn't look very happy, though, so maybe he hadn't offered a very good price?

Callie heard her name and saw Dorothea Finster waving at her from the stairs. The elderly owner of Haywood Hall looked excited, with spots of color on her cheeks. Callie rushed up to meet her. "Is something the matter?"

"I just wanted to take a moment to say how much I appreciate all of this. You put together such a wonderful program. The house is alive with people, music, flowers." She gestured around her. "Valentine's Day is a day of love, and I feel that love everywhere!"

Just as she said it, Mrs. Forrester burst from the library's door, holding scissors clutched in her hand like a weapon. Her face was pale with anger, and her eyes flashed as if she could barely control herself. She was so completely not a picture of love that, after Dorothea's adoring words, Callie almost had to laugh.

But something in Mrs. Forrester's expression prevented her from it. The woman was truly mad into the depths of her veins and ready to stab someone with those scissors, it seemed.

Dorothea glanced after her as she passed them and vanished down the corridor. "She's very good at what she does," she said weakly, almost as if to offer an excuse for the presence of the unpleasant woman on the premises.

"I guess," Callie said, to be accommodating, "that she has to be firm in order to run the library and all the other things she's involved in. She does get a lot done."

They looked at each other and then, in spite of herself, Callie had to laugh anyway.

Dorothea joined her, a soft chuckle behind a politely raised hand. "I would never have admitted it otherwise," she whispered, "but now I will tell you I am positively afraid of that woman. She is like a battle ram. When she comes for you, you'd better step aside or you'll get run to the ground. I wouldn't like to get into an argument with her."

"You're the hostess, so she won't pick a fight with you," Callie assured her. "Apparently she's very much a perfectionist, and when something doesn't turn out the way she had pictured it, she's none too pleased." She thought a moment. "Maybe she feels like everybody takes her efforts for granted."

Dorothea nodded, suddenly perfectly serious. "It can be a risk when you rely on the same people over and over to make every community event into a success. They are eager and pull their weight, but after a while they ask themselves what for. I must remember to give her an extra compliment when we're done later today. Can you help remind me?"

"Of course." Callie smiled at her. "We did intend to give all the volunteers a check for a free cup of coffee at Book Tea, so Mrs. Forrester will also be getting that."

"A lovely idea." Dorothea patted her arm. "I'm so glad to have you here. Oh . . ." She pointed at the grandfather clock. "It's almost time for the performance. Are you coming too?"

Callie hesitated. She wanted to hear the enigmatic Sean Strong sing, but she also felt obliged to keep an eye on how things were going. "You go and I'll pop in later," she said to Dorothea, who nodded and slowly made her way down the stairs. She didn't look like she was ninety-three, but Callie imagined she could feel it in her bones.

With a warm smile, she followed the fragile figure as Dorothea made her way down and then turned to the ballroom. Music already poured out the door, inviting people to flock there. Groups of chatting women and a few men came from the drawing room, some still carrying their coffee cups, and headed over. Callie caught a glimpse of Iphy at the door into the drawing room. She seemed to stand there very still, listening to the music, even closing her eyes a moment as if to soak it up. She looked younger and very expectant. But then she turned away and went back into the drawing room, apparently determined to stay at her post.

Chapter Three

Callie had managed to catch the last bit of the performance, and she had to admit that Sean Strong had a wonderful voice. He carried them away from the ballroom, across the sea to the mountains and deserts he sang about, conjuring up blossoming flowers or snow and ice at a rise or fall of his voice. People swayed, tapped, and hummed along, and the whole room seemed to be full of the energy the lone singer projected as he stood there and filled the space with his voice. Warm applause reached out to him, and people called for an encore.

Callie saw that Quinn had come to stand with Peggy, who, like herself, had caught the closing part of the performance, and he now put his hand on her arm and asked her something. She seemed a bit surprised and hesitant, but followed him through the doors that led outside. Callie wondered if Quinn would tell her about the retriever puppies and ask her if the boys could have one. Peggy might not be eager for the extra responsibility, and Callie could only hope that a disagreement about it wouldn't ruin this otherwise nice day.

Sean Strong hushed the crowd with a hand gesture and launched into one more song. To Callie's surprise it wasn't a classical song, but a sweet, simple folk song, maybe Irish, about a girl he had once loved and how they had walked the country roads together, hand in hand, the sun on their faces and love in their hearts. Everybody listened, spellbound, as he asked her why she had gone away and left him with nothing but the memories of those sun-soaked days. A woman rubbed her eyes, and even Callie felt a bit of tightness in her throat as Strong seemed to live the words he sang, putting his all into the lines, into the vibrations of his rich voice.

It was very silent when he finished. Then people rose to their feet and applauded him even more fervently than before.

Callie turned and saw Iphy standing at the door of the room. She turned away quickly, but Callie had glimpsed the emotion on her face—a tenderness and sadness she had never seen there before. Iphy stood motionless, seemingly almost forgetting she was in a room full of people, until someone pushed past her, and she excused herself. Callie didn't want to go to Iphy and intrude on what seemed to be a personal moment. After all, she knew so little about her great-aunt's life—whether she had ever loved, hoped to marry and have a family, only to see that hope swept away from her when love had been lost. Lost in death? Lost to life? Callie didn't know. She went outside, allegedly to check on her car, which she knew was locked up tight, but just to get away for a moment and collect her thoughts. To her surprise, she caught Peggy running to her own car and fidgeting to get the door open. When Callie drew closer, she saw Peggy's shoulders were shaking. She realized with a shock that her friend was crying.

"Peggy!" She went over quickly. "What's wrong?"

"Just leave me alone. Let me go. How can he . . . how can he ask me that?" Peggy had the door open, dove into the car, and started the engine even before she had buckled up.

Callie tapped on the window, wanting to tell her she was in no state to drive. But Peggy took off anyway, breezing down the driveway to the exit.

Callie blinked in confusion. Was it about the puppy? Asking someone to get a dog they might not want to take on right now didn't warrant such an emotional response, did it? What was the matter here?

She brushed her forehead, turning away, when she saw Quinn coming. His hair stood up as if he had raked it back with this hands, and his eyes looked frantic. He called, "Did you see Peggy?"

"She drove off." Callie took a deep breath. "I think she was crying."

Quinn halted. His shoulders sagged, and he looked at the ground. He exhaled long and hard. "I shouldn't have . . ." He seemed to mutter more under his breath.

Callie went over to him. "Did you argue? I've never seen her like that."

Quinn looked up at her. "I'm sorry, I can't talk about it." He turned away, breaking into a trot.

Callie blinked. *Well, I never. It's like people aren't themselves today.*

"Callie!"

She turned at the urgent voice. It was Mrs. Moffett, Mrs. Forrester's right hand at the library. They were so often seen together that some locals mockingly called Mrs. Moffett "The Shadow." In contrast with her formidable boss, she was a soft-spoken personality who often excused herself when she hadn't done anything wrong. She looked frantic as she ran for Callie. Her heart-shaped badge had almost come loose and dangled from her lapel. "It is—oh, it's terrible. I don't know what to do."

"What's terrible?" Callie asked, catching the woman by the shoulders to steady her. She seemed to be swaying as she tried to catch her breath. Mrs. Moffett blinked her wide green eyes at her. "I should never have gone in there alone. But I saw him go in there. I thought he might still be there. I only wanted to ask if he might do a few more evaluations. Just because there were so many people, and I hate disappointing—" She gasped for breath.

"Take it easy now," Callie said soothingly. "It will be all right."

"No, it won't." Mrs. Moffett pushed the next few words out with an effort. "He's dead."

"Dead?" Callie echoed. Surely not another dead body at Haywood Hall. Everything inside her resented ever living through something like that again.

"Dead?" Callie repeated once more. "You must be mistaken. You must have seen something, perhaps in the dimness of that room." Yes, that was it! A trick of the eyes or the mind.

But Mrs. Moffett shook her head emphatically. "He's dead! He's lying on the floor. Staring up at the ceiling. He looked kind of surprised. Like he couldn't believe someone had dared to kill him. And there was blood nearby—oh!"

She held her hand to her mouth. She kept her panicky eyes on Callie. "I know we all said that someday she'd kill someone. She's fierce like that. But I never meant it. Not like she would really do it. Not—" She gasped again.

Callie squeezed her shoulders. "Calm down now. Who's dead?"

"Our expert. Mr. King. I would never have guessed you could kill a tall, strong man just like that. He stood two heads over her! Maybe she never intended to. Maybe she just wanted to threaten him to put him in his place. And then—" Mrs. Moffett sucked in air. "It's too horrible."

Callie said, "Are you certain that there is a dead body?"

Before she could say more, Iphy appeared by her side. "People are saying there's something wrong upstairs. Someone hurt or even dead. We should go up and have a look before things get out of hand."

"Mrs. Moffett here says she's seen it." Callie swallowed. "Another murder."

Iphy brushed her forehead. "That can't be. Who would kill someone on such a nice day? A perfectly harmless event?"

Callie tried not to think of Iphy's own strange response to the appearance of Sean Strong, Peggy's tearful departure, Quinn's tension earlier, and Mrs. Forrester holding the scissors like she could just . . .kill someone with them.

Yes. There had been a positively murderous look in her eyes.

Telling herself not to draw any hasty conclusions, Callie focused on Mrs. Moffett. "We have to call the police."

"You do it." Iphy nodded at Callie. "I'll go in with Mrs. Moffett, and we will make sure nobody gets into that room. We don't want people, especially children, seeing anything gruesome."

Mrs. Moffett whimpered as if she now realized it was too late for her, and she had already seen the gruesome thing. Iphy put a firm arm around her and led her away.

Callie dug her phone from her pocket and hesitated a moment. The police station or Deputy Ace Falk's cell phone? She had his number because he was . . .

Sort of her boyfriend?

Callie frowned as she didn't really want to think about that issue right now. They were going out together every now and then, to have dinner or see a movie; they were having a good time together, having serious conversations or just talking about nothing really; and just feeling that they liked to be together. So why did she have to wonder why he had never officially asked her to be his girlfriend? Or why they were always going to other towns on their dates, almost as if they shouldn't be seen together around Heart's Harbor?

Not to mention that after the sheriff's unfortunate concussion on New Year's Eve, Ace had been so busy leading things at the station that she had barely seen him at all.

Callie shook her head. She didn't need him privately now, but for business. Another murder case where she happened to be on the scene. How did that keep happening to her?

She chose his cell phone number from her contact list and waited as the phone rang.

"Hello?" She could hear wind blowing past the receiver, so she knew he was outside. Maybe on some case looking at evidence or searching for a fugitive?

"Ace? It's me, Callie. I'm at Haywood Hall for our Valentine's event, and someone . . . died here."

There was a short silence. "Died? You're serious?"

"Yes, unfortunately I am. Mrs. Moffett just came to tell me. An expert we asked to come evaluate old books died, and Mrs. Moffett is certain he was murdered. I haven't seen the body so I can't tell."

"And you are not going to see the body either. Stay away from it, please." Ace sounded pleading. "I will come over right away. You know the drill. No touching, no interfering. And nobody leaving."

Callie thought of Peggy, who had rushed off in tears moments before they had heard about the murder, but she didn't want to tell Ace that Peggy was upset about something—or rather, someone—and that someone was Quinn.

When Quinn had first come to town, Ace had been suspicious of him, and Callie didn't want the protective deputy to think that Quinn had somehow hurt his sister. Ever since Peggy had lost her husband and was raising her sons alone, Ace had tried to do anything he could to help them, and he would never allow anyone to harm them in any way. Callie was sure Quinn hadn't meant to hurt Peggy either, but still, she had raced off in a state of great distress.

What a mess!

"Callie?" She heard Ace's voice with an urgent undertone.

"Yes, I heard what you said, and I understand. I'll see you later." She disconnected and went inside to tell everyone to stay put as the police were coming in for an investigation of what had happened in one of the upstairs rooms. She wasn't going to call it a murder right away, but deep down inside she knew it could hardly be anything else. So much for their celebration of love.

Chapter Four

When Callie heard the sirens outside, she headed into the hallway to meet Ace the moment he came in. As always it struck her how capable he looked in uniform, how determined. But the moment their eyes met, she saw the concern for her there and the disbelief that murder had found their little town again. He came over with long strides, his hand reaching out as if he wanted to wrap an arm around her. Then he seemed to remind himself he was on duty and stood stiff and straight in front of her. "Where's the body?"

"Upstairs. I'll take you to it."

They walked up the carpeted steps, and as they went, she felt his hand brush hers a moment. "Are you okay?" he asked softly.

"Yes, I'm fine. Like I said, I didn't see the body, so it was just the shock of hearing that someone had died. The event was . . . well, rife with tension might be a bit much to say, but I did notice some people behaving oddly."

"Good, keep that in mind to tell me later. Every little detail might turn out to be important. These events with lots of people around are, of course, a nightmare for a police investigation. So many fingerprints around, traces—Forensics won't be happy." Ace glanced at her. "I'll take a look at the body first and talk to the person who found it."

"Mrs. Moffett," Callie said with a sigh. "You know her and how people even call her "The Shadow." She doesn't like being in the spotlight. And she's so upset, I wonder if you'll get much out of her."

"How did she happen to stumble upon the body? Did she tell you?"

"I had the impression she wanted to ask Mr. King a question and went into a room she had seen him enter earlier. There he was, dead on the floor." She frowned hard. "She mentioned something to me about her never having believed *she*—meaning some other woman—was capable of killing. That she looked fierce enough for it, but still . . ."

"She? The killer is a woman? Did Mrs. Moffett see her? Perhaps she noticed a woman exiting the room just as she approached to find this expert and ask her question?"

"Possibly. I have no idea who she meant." As Callie said it, she knew it wasn't the absolute truth. It made sense to think Mrs. Moffett would speak of someone she knew well. Was there anyone she knew better than her boss at the library, Mrs. Forrester? And Mrs. Forrester had been waving those scissors like . . .

Callie shook her head. No need to speculate. Mrs. Moffett would tell Ace exactly what she had seen. Then he could draw his own conclusions.

They came to the top of the stairs, and Callie looked in both directions. She saw Iphy and Mrs. Moffett down the corridor to her left, waiting in front of a door. Apparently that room had been assigned to Mr. King to put his things in and retreat to when he needed a break. Mrs. Forrester had taken care of that.

So she had known exactly where to find him alone?

Callie shook her head at her own morbid thoughts. She waved Ace along to the two waiting women. Mrs. Moffett stood with her head down, sobbing into her hands.

As Callie approached, she heard Iphy say, "You will have to tell him everything. There is no other way."

Callie's heartbeat stuttered. Had Mrs. Moffett considered holding something back from the police, from Ace? Why? Did she know more about the death than she wanted to admit?

Or was she considering shielding someone?

If she had really seen Mrs. Forrester leave the room right before she had gone up to the door . . .

Her boss, someone she had worked with for many years. Someone she might consider a friend, even though she was a bit dominant. Not a likeable personality, but not exactly a cold-blooded criminal either.

What a dilemma to face.

"Good afternoon, Mrs. Moffett," Ace said in a kind tone. "I heard you had quite a shock."

Mrs. Moffett looked up at him and rubbed her nose with her soggy handkerchief. "That's right, Deputy. I feel all shaky. I don't know quite what to say or do."

"How about you tell me slowly, and step by step, what happened this afternoon?" Ace suggested. He had produced a notebook and pen, and eyed the woman expectantly.

Iphy said, "Really, Deputy, she's had quite a lot to work through and is barely able to stand up. Can't we sit down somewhere quiet to talk?"

Ace looked over his shoulder and called out to one of his men. When he approached. Ace instructed, "In there is the body. Don't let anyone in except for the doctor as soon as he arrives. I'll speak to this prime witness first."

Mrs. Moffett shrank under the words *prime witness* and looked at Callie with wide, tear-stained eyes, pleading for help. She was obviously not used to being the center of attention, and certainly not a focal point for the police.

Callie put her hand on the woman's arm. "Iphy is right—you need to sit down. Let's go into this room." Being familiar with Haywood Hall's layout, she took Mrs. Moffett to the nearby billiard room and opened the door for her.

Ace, who followed them closely, whistled as he stepped inside. "I'd love to lay down a game of pool here some time."

Callie shook her head at him, as this was hardly the time to discuss something like that, but to be honest, she'd love to play pool with him, and especially here. She didn't claim to be very good at it, but she had played it quite a few times at hotels that had a billiard table, and she enjoyed the game.

Most of all, she enjoyed beating men who believed women couldn't play pool. She didn't want to say Ace would have such prejudices, but even so . . .

Mrs. Moffett sank into one of the three leather chairs grouped around the fireplace and buried her face in her hands again. Her shivery breathing filled the silence.

Iphy, who had come in with them, stood beside her and rested her hand on her shoulder. She looked at Ace and mouthed, "Easy does it."

Ace nodded with a reassuring look and sat down opposite the two women. He rested his notebook on his knee and said, "You were here to assist with the book part of the event, Mrs. Moffett?"

"Yes." Mrs. Moffett lifted her head. "It's called Fall in Love with Books, and we thought up such good ideas for it. We're doing a book swap, you know, where you can exchange a book you've read for something new, and we had this expert come over to determine the value of old books. Mr. King came in rather late, and he was quite demanding. I thought to myself, *His name is King and he behaves like a king, expecting us to run for him at his every beck and call.* I wouldn't let him know how I felt, of course. He was our guest of honor. Mrs. Forrester has talked about him incessantly since asking him to come over and him agreeing. He had a young man with him who helps him. I can't remember his name. But he is very efficient. And not at all stuck up like Mr. King was."

Ace took notes. "You met the expert on his arrival?"

"No, Mrs. Forrester handled that. She was very proud of herself that she had signed him up for the event. He's on TV sometimes, you know, in one of those shows where people bring in buys from junk sales, hoping they turn out to be a real antique treasure. I bet if I tried it, mine would be worth nothing. But sometimes you see people get the news they really have something big."

"I think I saw a bit of that once," Ace said in a pleasant, conversational tone. "Those experts really know their stuff."

Mrs. Moffett nodded and sat up. "He was supposed to be the afternoon's star attraction."

Callie tried to keep a straight face, as she was certain the musical bit with baroque orchestra and famous baritone had been advertised as the event's highlight, but apparently Mrs. Forrester had liked to think she had brought in the main star.

"I have to admit," Mrs. Moffett said in a tone as if she was sorry, "that it got on my nerves how she went on about him, especially after I saw him in the flesh." She twisted her soggy handkerchief. "He was a rather ordinary man with dyed hair, you know. In fact, nothing about him seemed particularly real."

She frowned hard. "Even his signet ring struck me as bought from a site to engage in those live role-plays where everyone is a knight, highwayman, or princess with ladies-in-waiting. My grandson is completely wrapped up in that world. He has a collection of medieval swords and things, all replicas of course."

"Of course." Ace nodded. Callie bet he was slightly confused by this sidetrack but didn't want to pull the woman back to the facts with a direct question. She seemed to forget about her shock a little now that she was telling her side of it, and he obviously wanted her to keep going. Mrs. Moffett said, "I thought he was rather stuck up and unreal, but Mrs. Forrester praised him to me and to his face. It was rather embarrassing how she tried to please him, offering him a room where he could retreat if he wanted to. And he just looked at her down that long nose of his as if he was laughing at her secretly. It was very unpleasant."

She shivered. "I was glad I didn't have to work with him, like that poor young man. Just before it started, he yelled at him. Really yelled at him. Not spoke with a raised voice, no—shouting. And cursing too. Such an unpleasant character."

She crossed her arms over her chest, and then suddenly her expression fell. Her features crumpled, and she gasped, raising a hand to her lips. "And now he's dead. I'm so sorry. One shouldn't speak ill of the dead, of course."

"On the contrary, Mrs. Moffett," Ace said quietly, "it can really help if you paint me as complete a picture of the deceased as you possibly can. I do understand you hardly knew him, but you seem very observant, and every tiny bit of information can help solve this crime."

Mrs. Moffett relaxed a bit. "Oh," she said as if she couldn't grasp the concept of her story being important. "Oh."

A flush of gratitude or actual excitement rose in her cheeks. "I see." She sat up again. "Well, he shouted at that poor young man because of something he hadn't put ready on the table. A loupe or something. And that young man shrank and crouched behind the table to look for it. It was like he wanted to crawl into a corner. So very sad for a grown man, don't you think? I remember saying to myself that it had to be very crushing for one's self-esteem to work for someone who is always finding fault."

Callie wondered a moment if Mrs. Moffett knew this from her own experience. After all, Mrs. Forrester could also be considered someone who always looked for and found shortcomings in her fellow beings.

Ace nodded. "So this expert was a man who looked down on other people, you'd say."

"And grossly overrated his own talent." Mrs. Moffett nodded and leaned over as if she wanted to share something highly confidential. "He gave ridiculously low values to those books. I'm no expert myself, but I felt like those people were really robbed."

Callie looked at Iphy, who shook her head as if to indicate that Mrs. Moffett had to be in the wrong here. After all, people usually thought their old stuff was worth much more than it turned out to be.

"He sat down to work then, and there were people around, so no harm came to him there," Ace said.

"Certainly not," Mrs. Moffett said with a snort. "When he left the room, he was alive and well, bumping into someone, almost stepping on their foot and not even excusing himself."

"So he left for a short break—and then?"

"He didn't come back." Mrs. Moffett widened her eyes. "Mrs. Forrester went after him, but even she couldn't persuade him to come back. And then . . . he was dead. I found him. I didn't go near him, I didn't touch anything. But the way he lay there . . . Nobody lies on the floor like that. I ran out again, and I looked for Callie to tell her about the dead body."

Ace's eyes narrowed. He seemed to clutch his pen. "Why Callie? Why not Mrs. Forrester?"

Mrs. Moffett looked startled. "I . . . uh . . . I thought I should report to one of the organizers of the event."

Callie tilted her head, unsure what it was in the woman's tone that didn't strike her as genuine. Was she fudging the truth?

"Where was Mrs. Forrester at that time?" Ace asked.

Mrs. Moffett smoothed her wet handkerchief. "I have no idea. I ran down and found Callie and told her what I had seen. She asked me to wait inside with Iphy while she called you." Mrs. Moffett exhaled as if she was glad to be done. "Can I go now? I have a terrible headache and want to lie down in my own bed."

"Just a few more questions. You've already helped me so much." Ace smiled. "When you went to the room where you expected the expert to have retreated, did you see anyone coming from that direction? Someone who might have been in there with him?"

"No." The answer came fast. "The corridor was empty."

"Are you sure?" Ace leaned over closer to her. "You saw no one? Not even a shadow? Someone going down the other direction?"

Twisting the handkerchief into a knot, Mrs. Moffett took a deep breath. "I did hear the click of a door closing. So maybe the killer hid in one of the other rooms while I came over." She swallowed hard. "I'm glad I didn't run into him. He could have killed me too."

"Him?" Ace queried. "You think it was a man?"

"Why, yes, the expert was a tall man, not very broad in the shoulders maybe, but wiry. He could have defended himself. I can't see someone killing him unless it was a man. A strong man."

Callie looked at Mrs. Moffett closely, suspicion niggling inside. Earlier she had told Callie something about a *she* who might have killed. Now she insisted it had to have been a man. Why?

Ace played with his pen. "I don't know how the murder was committed, so I have to keep all options open. Supposing it could also have been a woman . . . Did you see or notice anything? Maybe the scent of perfume in the room when you walked in? Scents can be pretty pervasive."

"Or perhaps I saw a brooch that had fallen to the floor?" Mrs. Moffett laughed nervously. "No, no such thing. I can't remember the scent of the room. I just saw a dead man, and I panicked and ran. I really want to go home now."

Her voice trembled, and Ace closed his notebook and got up. "Of course, Mrs. Moffett. I think Iphy can take you and make sure you're all right."

Iphy nodded at him gratefully and led the woman to the door.

As soon as the two were gone, Ace looked at Callie. "What do you think?" Before she could answer, he said, "I let you and Iphy be there because she was upset, and if you had left, she might have clammed up, but I don't intend to involve you in this case in any way. Twice was enough, you know."

Callie nodded. "Of course. I think she was really very upset. It's hard to tell if she was just incoherent because of her mood or if she was . . ."

"Lying?" Ace pointed his pen at her. "I had the distinct impression she did see someone before she entered the room. But she can't believe that person to be involved in something as gruesome as murder, and therefore she's denying it. But that could be dangerous. People who killed once usually don't hesitate to kill again if they believe a witness can identify them."

Callie wanted to say something about that but was interrupted by a knock on the door. A man dressed in white poked his head around the door and said, "We have fingerprints on the murder weapon. A perfect set."

"What's the murder weapon?" Ace asked, his pen poised to write it down in his notebook.

"A pair of scissors."

Callie gasped. Ace glanced at her and then waved away the man in white. "I'll be there in a minute." He focused on Callie and said, "What is it? The mention of scissors seems to have spooked you."

Callie shrugged. "Earlier this afternoon I saw Mrs. Forrester walking around with a pair of scissors in her hand, clutching it like it was a weapon. She seemed deeply upset about something."

Ace nodded. "If she was holding the scissors, that explains her prints on them." He waited a moment. "Still, it puts her in an awkward position. She asked this expert to come here, so she knew him on some level. I mean, it is more likely that she would get into conflict with him than a perfect stranger here at the event."

Callie nodded. "That seems logical, yes. I'm worried . . ." She fell silent and looked for the right words.

Ace waited patiently, his dark eyes scanning her expression.

"Yes?" he prompted.

"I really don't know for sure and shouldn't—"

"Tell me. Your gut feeling has been right before."

"It's not a gut feeling even. When Mrs. Moffett approached me and reported the murder, she seemed to think Mrs. Forrester had committed it. She referred to someone who was fierce and insistent but need not be capable of killing. She must also have seen Mrs. Forrester rushing around with the scissors."

Ace nodded. "If she caught a glimpse of them in the victim, she could have drawn a quick conclusion."

Callie studied his features. "And what conclusion are you drawing?"

"That I need to speak to Mrs. Forrester."

Ace walked to the door. He hesitated with his hand on the knob. "I do realize one thing."

"What's that?"

"I asked Mrs. Moffett why she reported the murder to you and not to her boss, Mrs. Forrester. She said it was because you're one of the organizers, and of course that might make total sense. Besides, it would be normal not to act perfectly logically, as she was startled and running away from a dead body she had stumbled on. But still, can't we also guess that the reason she didn't want to tell Mrs. Forrester about the dead body was that she suspected her of being the killer and couldn't see herself reporting a murder to the actual murderer?"

A chill went down Callie's spine at the idea.

Ace held her gaze as he continued. "Mrs. Moffett might have been afraid that if she faced Mrs. Forrester, the woman would sense her suspicions, and that would not exactly be smart. Or safe."

Callie licked her lips. "You have to speak to Mrs. Forrester and clear this up. I mean, we can't have . . ." She reached up and rubbed her forehead.

Ace came over and smiled at her, a sad smile. "It's happened again, Callie. And this time you're not going to be helping me. It wouldn't be right. We're . . ." He waited and seemed to look for the right word. "Well, you know."

And he vanished out of the door.

Callie stared at the closed door, wishing he had ended his sentence and put a word to what they actually were. Just dating, feeling out the possibilities of a relationship? Or were they in a relationship? To her it was definitely the latter, but Ace always seemed a bit more reserved. Was it just because he was so insanely busy after the sheriff's concussion, so personal stuff was the last thing on his mind? Or was something else holding him back?

Callie shook her head with a rueful smile. Whatever Ace was thinking, the murder had thoroughly ruined their chances for a romantic Valentine's Day.

Chapter Five

Callie was packing the last of their tea supplies into boxes when Ace came into the drawing room. He walked upright as always, but Callie could tell by the tightness in his shoulders that he was feeling the pressure of having to organize everything, speak to people, take initial statements, and make decisions about what to do next. He halted and looked at her with a frown, obviously trying to determine something. Then he asked, “Where’s Peggy? She was here working with you to serve tea and cookies all afternoon, right?”

Callie nodded. “She was here before.”

She wasn’t sure she should tell Ace about the state in which Peggy had left the premises, so she decided not to underline the point unless Ace specifically asked about it.

Ace stood and looked about him as if he expected to find Peggy. “I haven’t seen her anywhere. Are you sure she’s all right? The boys are in the stables with Quinn, but they don’t seem to know where she is either.” Worry furrowed between his eyes. “I called her cell phone, but she’s not answering.”

Callie's stomach squeezed. She should have gone after Peggy or at least tried to ensure in some way that she was all right. She checked her watch. It had been hours since Peggy left.

Ace asked, "Do you have any idea where she might be?"

"No." Callie came to a decision. It was better if she talked to Peggy before Ace did, and Quinn got into trouble. "I'll go to her house and see if she's there. If it's okay for me to leave."

"Yes, I don't think you killed Mr. King." Ace's tired expression relaxed a moment. Then he asked, "Why would Peggy have gone home? Without telling anyone? Was she feeling unwell? And why wouldn't she answer her phone?"

"Just let me go over to her house, and I'll call you with news as soon as I can."

Callie wanted to walk past him to the door, but Ace grabbed her arm. "Do you know something? Is she sick? Has she been keeping that from me?"

Callie shook her head, but Ace pressed her wrist harder and said, "Don't keep things from me, Callie, please. I know if Peggy asked you to keep something a secret, you'll feel loyal to her and all that, but she's my sister. I love her, and I would do anything for her."

Even turn against me, Callie mused, and then rebuked herself for this irrational, unkind thought. Ace was handling a murder investigation here and was suddenly confronted with his missing sister and a suspicion of why she had left without saying something to anyone. That would of course prompt questions.

"I don't know anything about her being ill. If I did, I would have told you. I'll just go to her house and let you know right away what's up. Promise."

Ace let go of her and sighed. "Sorry, Callie, I just . . . Another murder, in our town. People being upset and afraid and asking me what's happening, and the sheriff still being incapable of doing much. That stupid accident on New Year's Eve. I still can't figure out how you can hit your head on a beam in your own attic and get a concussion that keeps you out of work for weeks."

"Injuries to the head and neck are always tricky," Callie said. "People involved in rear-end collisions can sometimes suffer symptoms for months without doctors being able to find any clear sign of damage."

"Yeah, yeah." Ace made a dismissive gesture with both hands. "I've heard that from several people. Fact is, though, I'm left to fend for myself, and there were hundreds of people present on the grounds when this murder took place. Some job." He nodded at her. "You let me know about Peggy, huh?"

"As soon as I can. Scout's honor." Callie slipped out the door and felt in her pocket for her car key. She hoped with all her heart Peggy would be at home and was simply not answering her phone because she was upset and didn't want to talk to anyone.

But after a couple of hours, how upset could she still be?

With worry clawing at her stomach, Callie got into her car and drove away from Haywood Hall. Looking back at the majestic mansion in her rearview mirror, she noticed the

smoke she had seen on arrival was still cheerfully wafting from the chimneys. But now something had been added to the cozy sight—an incongruous element: police cars in front of the house. Even without their lights flashing, it made the place look like the scene of an accident.

But murder was no accident, Callie realized. It was deliberate. Mrs. Forrester? Irritated already, on edge because of the pressure of this big event she felt personally responsible for, confronted with the expert she had engaged who didn't treat her with respect but looked down on her—had he perhaps shouted at her like he had at his unfortunate assistant? A weapon at hand, a stab in red-hot anger, then panic. *"What have I done?"*

Callie swallowed as images of how it might have played out filled her head, and she clutched the wheel. She just hoped Ace would figure out how to handle this without jumping to hasty conclusions and—even worse—making impromptu arrests that could damage someone's good name and reputation forever. Callie wanted no part in this.

She would just make sure Peggy was okay and then . . . what? Forget about all of it?

She realized with a heavy feeling inside that it wouldn't be that easy, as Haywood Hall was part of her life here, her work, her everyday existence. She and Iphy had taken on the immense responsibility of preserving the house for future generations, at Dorothea Finster's explicit request.

Dorothea! Callie realized that she hadn't even had a chance to talk to the elderly lady and comfort her after the shock of another murder in her home. Again Mrs. Keats—the faithful

housekeeper, Iphy, and the Book Tea crew were all involved, if only by being near the scene as it happened. Thinking back to the first murder she had helped solve, she recalled vividly how hard it had been just because so many people she cared for had been under scrutiny and turning to her for help to clear their names.

The domineering Mrs. Forrester was no particular friend of hers, so she need not feel that same anxiety in this case, but she did realize that if the woman was innocent, her position was very precarious, and she had to be terribly afraid.

Callie turned into the road Peggy lived on and looked at the numbers. It was dusk already, and she almost turned into the wrong driveway. But then she saw Peggy's car. Did that mean she was at home? That would make it easy to check up on her and inform Ace that everything was all right.

With some relief, Callie parked her vehicle behind Peggy's car and got out, closing the door softly. She walked up to the house but didn't knock on the front door with the fishnets beside it and the little wooden boat that read on the bow "Greg Peggy Jimmy Tate," a bittersweet memory of Peggy's intact family before her husband's death.

She walked around back to where the kitchen was and looked in through the kitchen window.

For a moment Callie thought Peggy wasn't there, and she'd have to return to the front of the house anyway to ring the bell, but then she caught sight of her friend sitting at the kitchen table, her head supported in both of her hands. Callie felt relief rush through her that Peggy was there, and

pulled out her cell phone. She quickly texted to Ace: *Peggy at home. Am going in to talk to her. Everything okay.*

As she typed the latter, her heart clenched because she wasn't sure at all that everything was okay, but Ace had wanted to know where his sister was, and at least Callie had located her and could tell him she was safe in her own home. She'd have to find out more first before she could decide what to tell Ace about it.

Her heart sank, thinking she might have to keep something from him. He had asked her not to, pleading with her even, but what if Peggy shared something with her that was confidential, and . . .

This was going to be very complicated.

Callie took a deep breath and then knocked on the window. Peggy jerked upright. She seemed reluctant to even turn her head and see who was there. Her tight posture suggested she was contemplating getting up and running off again into a part of the house where she wouldn't be observed. But then she slowly turned around. Her face was pale, her eyes red from crying. She seemed relieved, though, that it was Callie looking in, and came to the back door at once.

Callie had expected Peggy to invite her in straight away, and was already mentally making tea for her distraught friend, but Peggy opened the door only an inch or two and said in a hoarse voice, "I feel terrible—just leave me alone."

"Why do you feel terrible? Is there anything I can do for you? Maybe make a cup of tea?"

Peggy seemed to want to say no and bang the door shut, but after a few moments' consideration, she sighed and opened the door wider. "Why not? I can't face the boys this way. They aren't with you, are they?" She peered into the garden worriedly.

"No, they're still at the Hall. Quinn is looking after them." Callie realized Peggy had no idea that a murder had happened there, but it didn't seem like a good idea to tell her now, and since the boys were taken care of, it couldn't hurt to tell her later.

Peggy didn't seem pleased, though, to hear that Quinn was with her children. She hesitated and said, "Maybe you should go get them."

"They'll be fine there a little longer. A cup of tea first, okay? I'd like some too." Callie stepped forward, and Peggy backed up to let her in, then walked into the kitchen ahead of her and sat at the table again.

Callie picked up the kettle and filled it with water from the tap. She glanced at Peggy and saw she was looking at a book she had open on the table in front of her. Not just a book, but a photo album. Her finger traced a picture as she sat there, small and lost.

Callie put the kettle on and then walked over to her. She came to stand beside her and looked down at the photo album. The picture Peggy was caressing with her fingertip was a photo of a radiant bride, a smiling groom beside her. They looked devastatingly young and eager for life, holding onto each other tightly.

Callie's throat constricted as she recognized Peggy's features in the bride's face and realized the groom had to be Greg, Peggy's deceased husband. She was sitting here looking at the happiness she had once had and lost. Callie put her hand on Peggy's shoulder and said, "I'm here for you if you want to talk about it."

Peggy didn't say anything. She just kept stroking the image of her dead husband.

Callie had no idea how grief like that felt. She had never lost anyone that close to her. She still had both her parents, and she had never had a partner, let alone a husband. Thinking of Ace, she tried to imagine what it would be like to be married to him, have children with him, and then lose him, perhaps as he got shot in the line of duty. The news, the numbness, the shock, the loss, the loneliness. The struggle to get back on her feet, for the children's sake.

Even though thinking of Ace getting shot hurt like crazy, Callie was well aware that she couldn't imagine at all what it would be like to lose someone you had been living with for years and had built your entire existence around. It seemed surreal.

Peggy said in a hoarse voice, "I can't do it, Callie. I can't."

Callie squeezed her shoulder. She struggled with her need to say something comforting, but didn't know what, as she had no idea what Peggy was going through. She didn't want to say something superficial, shallow, or unfeeling.

Or, worst of all, clichéd.

She just stood there and listened to Peggy's breathing in the silence. Then the kettle began to sing, and she rushed to collect a teapot and mugs, tea bags, and cookies. At last she put down the teapot with brewing tea and a mug by Peggy's side and sat down opposite her. Still she hadn't said a word.

Peggy looked up at her. Her left hand found the mug and closed around it because she wanted to feel its searing warmth. "I can't do it. I just wish that Quinn hadn't done that, hadn't said that. Now I'll have to tell him I can't see him anymore."

Her expression tightened, and Callie was sure she was going to cry again. Her heart clenched for her unhappy friend who so deserved a little joy in her life.

But Peggy controlled herself with the greatest effort and stared into her tea.

Callie wasn't quite sure what to make of what she had said but she did recall how nervous Quinn had been when she had met him. Today was Valentine's Day and—oh no.

Had he maybe expressed his feelings for Peggy, and . . .?

Callie stirred her tea, even though there was no sugar in it, and looked at the vortex her spoon formed all the way to the bottom of the mug.

"Why did he have to do that?" Peggy asked again. "It was going fine. Him coming here for dinner, playing with the boys, doing a chore here and there. Us having lunch when I came from Book Tea and him from the community center. It was all going fine."

Peggy's free hand formed into a fist. "He should just have accepted what he could get. Friendship. Being a part of something. Togetherness. The feeling life was getting better again. That it wasn't all cold again, but maybe could be a little warm and have some colors. But"—her fist banged the table—"he wanted more. Stupid . . ." She sucked in a breath.

Callie waited, still not sure how to respond. A thousand thoughts rushed through her head, but she couldn't decide which one was the right one.

If there even was a right one.

Peggy said, "I know it's Valentine's Day and all, but that didn't mean he had to—he even got me a present." Her voice broke, and she sobbed into her hands.

Callie took a sip of tea. It was so hot it burned her tongue. She put the mug down and ran her hand over the tablecloth.

"Nobody gets me presents like that since Greg died," Peggy said in a strangled tone. "When he gave it to me, it was like it was the old days again. Like I could be happy again. But that isn't right. It isn't." She pressed her clenched fist against her mouth.

Callie wondered if Quinn, on giving Peggy a present, had smiled and leaned down to kiss her. It seemed like a quite natural thing to do. But apparently it had totally unnerved Peggy. She hadn't seen it coming, or maybe, deep down inside of her, she had but had avoided thinking about it, confronting the issue.

Callie glanced at the photo album, the smiling couple looking out into a life together. Believing they could conquer it all as long as they held on tightly to each other.

She said, "How did you meet Greg anyway?"

Peggy looked up. A smile flickered over her exhausted features. "On the beach. He was surfing. He loved water. That's also why he joined the Coast Guard. The sea was everything to him. He never believed he could control her.

He always told me she was a fickle mistress, giving and taking as she wanted. He knew how dangerous it was. But he had to go anyway. That was just his way."

She smiled tenderly down at the wedding photo. "I knew when I married him that he might someday . . . you know, but you put it out of your mind. I was sure he was careful. Especially after the boys were born. He loved them to bits—he would never leave them."

She swallowed hard. "I'm sure Greg did everything he could to be safe during missions. But when there were lives at stake, he lost sight of his own safety. He wasn't reckless, but he also wouldn't hesitate to take a risk if he believed he could save a life."

She looked up. "He saved three teens that night. Silly kids had gone out in a boat, no idea of boating, no clue as to the weather or the undertow. Without Greg and his colleagues, they would have died for sure. Greg dove deep to drag up the third one. He'd heard it was dangerous because there was wind and the sea was so rough. But he had to do it anyway. He got hit by some planking."

Peggy sat there, the tears still on her lashes, her eyes staring into nothing. "They pulled the kid from his arms into the boat, and they wanted to grab Greg but he was losing consciousness because of the blow to his head or lack of oxygen from his deep dive, and he sank away before they could get him in. They did everything to save him, I'm sure, but it didn't help. I guess . . ."

Her expression was tender. "Greg died believing he had done the right thing. He couldn't help himself, I know, but it hurt." She looked at Callie, her eyes wide and childlike. "It hurt, Callie, and I can't go through that again."

Callie took a deep breath.

Peggy lifted her hand. "Just don't say anything, please. I know Quinn is a good guy and he loves the boys. I'm just not looking for a relationship. Not right now—maybe never."

She snapped the album shut and held it against her. "Thanks for coming over and asking if I was all right. I am. I will be. I just don't want to see Quinn right now. Could you go get the boys and bring them here?"

"Of course I can." Callie rose. "I do have to say that something happened at the Hall. The boys were nowhere near it, but the police are there to look into it. Ace—"

"Does Ace know about—?" Peggy seemed worried.

"No, just that you left. I'll tell him you had a headache." As soon as Callie said it, she realized she was agreeing to lie to Ace for Peggy. And that that would mean trouble sooner or later. "He might not believe it, but—"

"I'll call him." Peggy pulled out her cell phone. "I'll tell him I'm not feeling well and that you'll bring the boys to me. I don't want to see him here and get all these questions about what happened and how—he'll blame Quinn, and it's not Quinn's fault really."

Peggy raised the phone to her ear, and soon she was talking to Ace. Callie waited until she had finished and then took her leave, telling Peggy to lie down on the sofa a bit. "Drink that tea," she said, handing her the mug. "There's more in the pot."

"Thanks." Peggy held her gaze. "I don't want you to lie to Ace for my sake, but just try not to let him think any further than that I got a headache. He'll be knee deep in work anyway, I hope. He won't think too much of it."

Callie nodded and left the house. She hoped she could pick up the boys without running into Ace at all. In person, it would be harder to just pretend. There was nothing really wrong with Peggy, so it wasn't like she was hiding some terrible thing from him but still . . .

She almost wished she didn't know anything at all!

Chapter Six

Back at Haywood Hall, the number of parked cars had thinned out, suggesting people had been allowed to leave after providing their contact details and an initial statement about what they had heard or seen that could be related to the murder.

Callie believed that most people present had probably not noticed anything worthwhile and were just the unfortunate victims of a tragic death during a public activity.

She sighed, realizing how their Valentine's event would be remembered: as the one with the murder. *"You know, that man who got stabbed with scissors in the room upstairs?"* They had, of course, hoped their event would be memorable, but not in this way!

Callie went to the stables and found the volunteers from the shelter busy packing up everything they had brought to present the dogs to the public. The dogs themselves had already been put into the shelter vans, and the stables seemed oddly empty without their presence. Tate and Jimmy looked glum, sitting on a hay bale, kicking it with their heels. When they saw Callie, Jimmy called out, "Quinn won't let us take the puppy home. I bet if Mom saw him, she'd love him too and we could have him."

"A puppy is a lot of work," Callie said, closing in and smiling down on them. "Speaking of going home, it's time to go. Your Mom is home already, so let's go too."

"Why didn't Mom come see the puppy?" Tate asked, looking up at her with wide eyes. He enjoyed being the baby of the family and used his charm whenever he believed it could get things to go his way.

"Mom is very tired," Callie said. "I think it best to just come along now."

The boys sighed, but Jimmy pulled Tate to his feet and marched him off. Callie wanted to follow them but then saw Quinn standing there, looking at her much like Tate had. She wanted to avoid talking to him, but it was no use, as he was already closing in on her. "Is Peggy okay?"

"She just asked me to come get the boys and bring them home. I really don't know anything else," Callie said quickly.

"Come on," Quinn snorted. "You and Peggy are friends. She told you what happened, didn't she?"

"I only know she left and was quite upset. I didn't ask details." Callie pulled back her shoulders as if against an invisible accusation that she would have pried into someone's private affairs.

Quinn said softly, "Can't you guess? I fell in love with her the first day I met her, Callie. She's just perfect. Pretty, witty, fun to be with. I thought that spending time with her and the boys would make her see . . . Maybe she won't fall madly in love with me like she did with her husband. I know how much she loved him and probably still does. But he's gone. She needs a man, someone to be there for her and make her laugh. I want to be that man. I thought that after all the months we spent together, she'd care for me too. Just a bit, you know—a start. But when I kissed her, she acted like it was the most terrible thing I could have done."

Callie drew breath slowly. So that was it. Quinn had given Peggy a present and then, under the impression she shared his warm feelings, he had leaned in and kissed her. And Peggy hadn't expected it and felt guilty about her dead husband and had run off to hide away.

Quinn said, "I feel like a heel now. Like I forced myself on her or something. But I thought she cared for me too. I never thought it was like what she had with Greg because I know I can't compete with the man she's loved ever since she was a teenager. She had kids with him and all. But still, I believed we could have something different. That we could mean something to each other. Not that . . . she hated me."

"I'm sure she doesn't hate you, Quinn." Callie figured that if Peggy hadn't felt anything for Quinn, she would have told him so. She would have gotten angry rather than sad. It seemed like she did care for Quinn, in her own way, but felt like she shouldn't. That it was somehow wrong.

As Callie wasn't sure about this, she didn't want to put it into words, though and just said, "Give it some time, Quinn. Maybe Peggy didn't see it coming, and it just took her completely by surprise."

Quinn looked doubtful. "She can't have missed how things were between us. That we were growing closer."

"Maybe it was there, but she never consciously allowed herself to consider it. Then you come and—"

"Barge in," Quinn said ruefully. "Honestly, I thought it was the right moment, Callie. Valentine's Day just seemed perfect for it. I had rehearsed what I was going to say and . . ." He put his hand on her arm. "Can't you—since you're going to Peggy now—can't you put in a good word for me? Can't you tell her I never meant to hurt her feelings and I want to talk it over with her?"

Callie took a deep breath. "Why don't you call her in the morning or something? I don't know if it's a good idea if I talk to her now. She just wants to be left alone."

Quinn looked sad. "I understand." His shoulders slumped as he stepped away from her.

"Callie!" Jimmy appeared beside them and eyed her accusingly. "You said you wanted to take us home, and now you're not coming."

He looked up at Quinn, and his expression cleared. "Are you making a plan?" he asked, his voice high with excitement. "So we can have the puppy? You can convince Mom."

"Your Mom isn't feeling well right now," Quinn said. "We'll have to wait until she's better."

Callie hoped he wasn't just giving this advice to the boy but also taking it to heart himself. She said goodbye and waved in passing to a few volunteers, who gave her curious looks, and then exited the stables to find Ace there, waiting for her with Tate by his side.

"You run ahead to Callie's car," Ace said to the boys, "and we'll follow. Go on now."

Jimmy seemed puzzled, but he didn't ask. He yelled to Tate, "Race you!" and they were off, flailing their arms as they ran.

Ace said to Callie, "Is Peggy okay?"

"I thought she called you," Callie said innocently.

"Yes, she did, but what does that tell me?" He gave her a probing look from his deep brown eyes. "You saw her—you know more than I do about how she really is."

"She's fine. She just needs some time to . . ." Callie considered a moment. "Valentine's Day is just not easy for her." It wasn't really a complete lie.

Ace sighed. "Still, huh." He kicked a stone on the path. "You hear so many stories about working through grief, and sometimes it seems like it's all over and done with in a few months. People have new relationships, get married again. They can deal with their grief because they've forged new bonds that support them. But Peggy . . . Greg's death hit her hard and she doesn't want to let go of the past, it seems. I don't mean that in a condemning way, just that I worry for her sake. Greg's gone; he can't hold her and help her with the boys, and I'm just sad for her that she feels like she has to do it all alone."

Callie stared ahead as she asked, "So you would be open to her having a new relationship? I would have thought you would rather have her stay on her own."

"So I can be her hero?" It sounded challenging. "If you think that, you don't know me at all."

Callie halted and faced him. "Then tell me what to think."

Ace held her gaze, his features tight, as if he was looking for an answer. "I want Peggy to be happy again. But sometimes I wonder if she ever will be."

The wind played around them, and the darkness seemed to squeeze just a little tighter. Sometimes happiness seemed just out of reach, so tantalizingly close and yet too far away to ever grab hold of.

Ace seemed to shake himself. He put his hand under her chin and lifted her face a touch. "I'm sorry, Callie, that today ended this way. Go take the boys home now. I'll call you, okay?"

She nodded, and he let go of her and walked back to the house. As Callie watched him, a lone, straight figure in the night, she wanted to run after him and hug him, tell him he didn't have to do everything alone either. But she had a task to complete.

Impatiently, she turned to the waiting children.

* * *

When Callie arrived at the Book Tea, the lights on the second floor were on, suggesting Iphy was upstairs. Callie felt relieved and went around back, receiving a warm welcome from Daisy, who ran for her and pressed herself against her leg. Callie lifted the Boston terrier in her arms and cuddled her, saying, "Hello there, girl. I missed you so much. But it was far too crowded there for you, little one. You'd have felt unhappy. And then a murder. Again."

Daisy whined as if she understood perfectly and licked Callie's cheek. Callie carried her up the stairs to find her great-aunt sitting on the sofa with a faraway look on her face. She was still wearing her coat, as if she had come in and sat down right away, not stirring again. Looking at her quiet face, Callie had the unpleasant sensation that everyone was different that day than they usually were, and not in a good way.

She clutched Daisy tighter as she said, "Iphy? Is something wrong?"

Iphy shook herself and looked at her. "Wrong?" she repeated. "No, nothing is wrong."

Then a wry laugh formed round her lips. "If you can claim nothing is wrong when someone has just been murdered." She reached up and rubbed her face. "Mrs. Forrester is on the run."

"What?" Callie asked. She must have misheard.

"Her fingerprints were on the murder weapon, and several people heard her arguing with the expert. I don't know what about. But Falk decided he had to take her along to the police station for questioning. With an attorney present and all. She must have panicked at the idea of such formal steps or just the shame of being taken in by the police, and ran. Her car was missing from the lot."

"She must just have been too upset to think this through." Callie eyed Iphy. "It doesn't mean she's guilty, I suppose. Not that I know her all that well."

"Falk didn't immediately assume she was guilty either, but he had to put out an APB on her anyway. He can't just let her cross the state line and get away. Little old lady or not."

"So the police are actively looking for her now?" Callie could hardly imagine the prim and proper library volunteer as a fugitive.

Iphy nodded. "She will be mortified. She never even gets a parking ticket, and now this."

"Well, her sense of shame should be the last thing she worries about. How about the charges? I also saw her barging around with those scissors. And she was really angry about something. What if she gets charged for real and locked up?" Callie tried to imagine Mrs. Forrester behind bars but came up short.

Iphy nodded. "There is a real chance of that. Falk argues that a random visitor of the event would have had no reason to fight with Mr. King or hurt him. But Mrs. Forrester knew him to that extent that she had invited him here to do book appraisals, and he was a part of the proceedings in her bookroom—the Fall in Love with Books part of the event."

Callie hemmed. "Still, that doesn't prove a whole lot. Did she say anything to you? I mean either ahead or after the murder?"

Iphy shook her head. "I was so busy. I barely had time to see anyone, let alone have conversations." She looked down at her outfit. "Here I am, still in my coat." She laughed, a nervous, insincere laugh. "I'd better take this off and think about something to make for dinner."

Callie looked her over with a sharp observant glance. "Are you sure there's nothing wrong? You don't seem like yourself. Of course, murder is shocking, but Mrs. Forrester isn't a close friend of yours."

"I do know her from the days she was a little girl. She's younger than me, and I used to babysit her and her siblings. They were a wild bunch, mainly because of her older brother's silly ideas."

Callie ignored this fond reminiscing and tried to get a foot in the door with a tentative "But does it . . .?" She wanted to ask about the handsome baritone but didn't quite know how to put it.

Iphy raised a hand, cutting her off. "Some other time, Callie. I'm going to fix us dinner. It's late enough as it is."

Callie nodded. It was probably for the best. She wanted to come along into the kitchen to lend a hand, but Iphy waved her into a chair. "You must be exhausted. Sit down and put your feet up. I'll bring you a plate of hot food as soon as I'm done."

Callie felt awkward letting her great-aunt do all the work, but she suspected she wanted to be alone, doing something distracting, and so she just took the offer, sinking into a comfy chair and putting her feet on a stool. Daisy curled up in her lap and grunted in satisfaction. As Callie watched how the Boston terrier's eyes fell closed at once, she wished it was that easy for her to relax and get some rest. Her head seemed to be full of thoughts and considerations, about Quinn and Peggy, Ace, Iphy and Sean Strong, and—most of all—Mrs. Forrester on the run and the dead body in the upstairs room.

She must have nodded off anyway, for the sharp sound of the phone woke her with a jerk, and she reached for the receiver on the table beside her. "Book Tea, Callie Aspen."

Heavy breathing answered her down the line. Callie sat up straighter, thinking it was some crank caller. "Hello?" she asked sharply. "Who's there?"

"Hello," a thin voice said. "I can't talk now. But I have to meet with you. Iphy and you. You can help me. Please."

Callie clenched the receiver. "Who is this?"

"You know. What if they listen in, tap the line? They can do so much these days. I saw it all on TV. It seems surreal it's happening to me now. You must help me."

Callie wanted to say the name, but the other woman's tangible fear of being overheard rubbed off on her, and she just said, "Where?"

"Iphy knows the place. Just tell her that it's where we used to play hide and seek. She knows." Then the line went dead.

Callie stared at the receiver, barely believing she had received this most mysterious phone call. She then put it down and rose, Daisy in her arms, to head to the kitchen. Iphy was just chopping carrots and looked at her over her shoulder. "I told you I don't need help." It sounded so sharp it would normally have hurt Callie's feelings, but she was now on fire to tell Iphy about the call.

"Didn't you hear the phone ring? I answered it, and it was Mrs. Forrester. At least I think it was. She didn't want to say her name for fear of being overheard. She seems to think the police are tapping our line. She wants to meet us—she thinks we can help her."

"Help her with what?" Iphy asked, bewildered, a carrot in her one hand, a knife in the other.

"Getting cleared of suspicion, probably," Callie said. Her heart sank as she thought of having to sort through another murder case. It wasn't just hard work to figure out motives and track down people who might be involved, but it always seemed to touch on people you liked or cared for, and get you in an emotional jam. Right now, standing here, feeling the afternoon's rush in her feet and the heartache of Peggy's situation in her chest, going out to save Mrs. Forrester was the last thing she wanted to do.

But Iphy nodded firmly, dropped the knife and carrot, and reached behind her back to untie the laces of her apron and take it off. "Did she say where she is?"

"She didn't want to name the place," Callie said with a grimace, realizing just how cloak and dagger this whole thing was. "But she said you'd know. Where you used to play hide and seek."

Iphy looked at her with a hitched brow. "She said that?"

Callie shrugged. "What's so odd about that?"

Iphy shook her head. "I didn't think she would have remembered. I just told you how I used to babysit her and her brothers. They were a wild bunch. Always getting away from me and running into trouble. One afternoon they were gone again, and I had to find them. Against all instructions given by their parents, they had gone to the old cannery. It's an abandoned building where they used to can fresh fish and other seafood. It was closed down in the sixties and should have been demolished right after. But it never was, and local kids like to go there to play. I have no idea what's left of it today. But I know where it is, and that's what counts if we want to find Mrs. Forrester. Let's go."

Iphy dropped her apron on the table, turned off the stove, and rushed to get her coat.

Callie stood undecided. She had a sinking feeling that this could mean trouble. Mrs. Forrester was on the run, so if they went to meet her, was that aiding and abetting a fugitive?

And what would Mrs. Forrester expect of them? To help hide her from the police? What if Ace ever found out about that?

She could never face him again!

Iphy popped her head around the door and said, "If you don't want to come, you don't have to. I can do it alone." The head disappeared right away.

Callie sighed. If her great-aunt wanted to dive in and help Mrs. Forrester, she'd do it, no matter what the cost. And it would make Callie feel better if Iphy wasn't alone in that. She just couldn't let her great-aunt rush out to some meeting, at an abandoned building no less, and sit there and feel peaceful about it. Being there would be better.

She ran after Iphy. "Wait for me!"

* * *

The headlights of Iphy's car were the only light as they moved down the dirt road. It was full of potholes, and the car bumped and groaned in protest. Callie sat with her hands clutched round the car seat, holding her breath against the shocks that seemed to rattle every bone in her body. She tried to discern a building in the distance, but it was too dark to see anything. A shiver went down her spine at the idea of how isolated this spot was. Mrs. Forrester had of course wanted to be safe from the police looking for her, but still . . . Places like this creeped Callie out.

Iphy checked the rearview mirror. "Doesn't seem like anyone is following us."

"Why would anyone want to follow us down this horrible road that leads nowhere?" Callie queried.

"Mrs. Forrester was afraid the police were watching us, to find her. That makes total sense. If Falk thinks Mrs. Forrester might contact us, he could have someone watching the Book Tea and monitoring our every move. But it doesn't seem like we're being followed at all." Iphy nodded in satisfaction. "There's the building."

Callie could still barely discern anything, but Iphy steered the car with confidence into what had once been a parking lot and was now just a field full of weeds shaking in the breeze. She turned the ignition off and, with the headlights gone, it was suddenly overwhelmingly dark and lonely. Callie reached for Iphy, grabbing her arm. "Are you sure this is a good idea? I mean, I can understand Mrs. Forrester being careful, but this is ridiculous! We could have met at a roadside cafe or some place. This is just too creepy. I don't want to get out of the car."

Ignoring her protests, Iphy opened the glove compartment and pulled something out. A click, and bright light filled the car. "Flashlight," Iphy declared, clutching the handle. "Now come along. We'd better go see where she's hiding."

Goaded by her great-aunt's brisk determination, Callie got out of the car, feeling the weeds brush against her. Some reached up all the way to her waist, and she felt thorns attach themselves to her clothes. The frosty night air made her shiver, and she dug her leather gloves out of her coat pockets and wrapped her scarf more tightly around her head.

She walked carefully across the lot, using her gloved hands to detach herself from grasping brambles time and time again. Behind her, Iphy shone the flashlight on the building. It was a large stone structure with many cracked windows and an old wooden door that was secured with a rusty metal chain. The wind sang through the broken glass and around the chimneys, and Callie cringed under the ominous creaking emanating from within. "Are you sure it's safe to be here? Could it come down on us?" She glanced up cautiously.

Iphy didn't reply as she was shining her flashlight on the metal chain securing the door. "This seems to be locked still. So she didn't go inside the actual cannery. But where can she be? Temperatures are falling, and she'd be looking for shelter, I assume."

Iphy pressed her thumb against her lips, thinking hard. Callie just huddled in her scarf and hoped they could leave again soon.

Then Iphy's expression brightened. "Of course! That's why she reminded me of that afternoon when I had to find them here. The old keeper's cottage."

She gestured to Callie to follow her.

"What?" Callie asked. "Where's this cottage?" But her great-aunt already strode away.

They rounded the building, and Callie detected a large open area in the back, where half-decayed wooden crates leaned into one another. Something scurried away between them. Or were Callie's eyes deceiving her in the weak light?

To the left was a sagging cottage.

"There used to be a keeper here," Iphy explained in a whisper, "a sort of security guard, if you will, who had to make sure at night and on weekends that nothing was stolen. He lived here on the premises with his family. Once the building was abandoned, the kids from the village turned the keeper's house into a play area. They baked pancakes there and played board games on the floor. I found my fugitive charges here that afternoon. I bet Mrs. Forrester is in there right now."

Callie hoped she was, because the darkness and eerie atmosphere, coupled with the warning sounds as if the structure was about to collapse, strung her tight nerves to their breaking point. She worried that if something simply brushed her, she'd scream her head off.

Her hands formed into fists, and she followed Iphy, who marched ahead, holding up the flashlight. *Mrs. Forrester is accused of murder,* a voice whispered in the back of Callie's mind. *Falk thinks she stabbed someone to death. A big strong man, two heads taller than she was. Here you are, letting Iphy walk ahead of you. What if Mrs. Forrester is waiting there, armed?*

But if the woman was indeed a killer, why hadn't she just run and left the state before the police could get her? Why hang around here and invite locals to come to her? That made no sense.

But who said that killers were logical people? Sane people even? What if Mrs. Forrester had somehow lost it that afternoon and was now . . .

A killing machine?

Callie tried to laugh at her own macabre feelings. Of course, as a person with a normally uneventful life, Mrs. Forrester was just panicking now that she was suddenly under suspicion of a serious crime and the police wanted to question her formally. She was afraid of being locked up and not being able to clear her name. That was enough to drive any person into a frenzy.

Iphy pushed the door of the sagging cottage open. “Hello?” she called. “Anybody there? It’s me, Iphy. I’ve come to help you.”

Callie followed close behind her. She waited unconsciously for something to swoop at them from the darkness. She wished she had found something in the yard beside the abandoned building to use as a weapon of defense. Even a rusty shovel would have been better than nothing.

There was a deep silence inside, only broken by Iphy’s steps on the creaking floor. Then a figure darted for them. Her arm was outstretched, and Callie gasped, her heart rate shooting up so high in seconds that she could feel the blood pounding in her temples.

Then the figure hugged Iphy. “You came, oh, you came.”

“Of course I came.” Iphy patted the sobbing woman’s shoulders. “I came for you back then, Frederica, and I came for you now. You knew I would.”

Callie stood waiting as Iphy soothed the upset woman and then coaxed her into an old chair. As the light of the flashlight played across her features, Callie was shocked to see how much she had changed in a few hours. The confident woman with her criticism of the decorations that weren't classy enough was completely gone, and a stunned, frightened, elderly lady stared up at her with red-rimmed eyes.

Iphy said, "I'm sure nobody followed us here. You can tell us what happened. All of it." Mrs. Forrester wrung her hands. "If only I had never invited that man to the event." Her voice shook. "On TV at Christmas, he seemed so nice—a real gentleman. I admired him. I thought he was . . ."

She swallowed hard. "He agreed to come free of charge. To help us with conserving Haywood Hall. For a good cause and all. But as soon as he had set foot there, had looked at the rooms—also rooms where he had no business—"

Her voice grew stronger as she recalled this behavior that had obviously enraged her. "He came to tell me he wanted a fee anyway. A steep fee because he had now seen that we could easily afford it. He said he had seen a vase he wanted. In exchange for his cooperation in the event. I was appalled. Outraged!" Mrs. Forrester waved both her hands to underline her point. "As if I can simply give away someone else's property. I told him that Mrs. Finster owned the house and all the things in it, and then he said he would find Mrs. Finster and tell her I had promised him the vase in return for his services. I said I had promised no such thing, but he just laughed at me and said he would produce an email in which

I had said it. I don't know how he thought to do that if I never sent him any such email, but I saw in his eyes that he meant it. I got so very, very cold inside."

Callie's gut squeezed as she looked at Mrs. Forrester and realized the predicament the woman had found herself in. Some stranger she had invited to their event accusing her, even implying he could make it look like she had given away someone else's property like a careless person, something she wasn't and would never be. Had it been enough of a motive for murder? A stab with the scissors in blind anger over his audacity?

Mrs. Forrester said, "We argued about it, and people must have overheard. Not the exact words, but raised voices. They will tell the police and then—"

"Your fingerprints are on the murder weapon," Callie said, "and because you ran, Falk also put out an APB on you."

Mrs. Forrester nodded. "I knew he would do that when I ran away from Haywood Hall. He'd have to. I don't blame him. But I just couldn't stay. I couldn't face the people and the shame of being arrested and taken along in handcuffs in front of people I've known all my life."

"Now you're on the run," Iphy pointed out gently. "That made it even worse."

Mrs. Forrester hung her head. "I know. That's why I called you. You have to help me. I never promised him any vase. Or anything else in the house. He agreed to come free of charge."

"Do you have an email from him saying so?" Callie asked.

"No, I wish I had. The initial contact was by email, but then he called me to talk about the details, and we agreed he'd come for free. Later I sent him directions to the Hall." Mrs. Forrester knotted her fingers. "I'm sure we never, ever discussed any precious vase from the Hall's collection."

"That vase is of secondary importance," Iphy said. "The main thing is, did you kill him?"

"Of course not. How can you think that of me?"

Iphy raised a placating hand. "I'm not thinking anything, I'm just putting the question you will have to face. The man is dead, and you argued with him shortly before he died."

"Yes, but I can't have been the only one who didn't like him. He was rude, pretentious, demeaning. There must have been others who hated him. One of them killed him at the event so there would be lots of people around, and it wouldn't be easy to establish who had done it." Mrs. Forrester looked pleading. "You must find out for me who did it. Please."

Iphy said, "When you left Mr. King after the argument about the vase he wanted to have, he was still alive and well?"

"Oh yes, he wanted to go and find Mrs. Finster to tell her about this fake email in which I had supposedly promised the vase to him. He had this mean, smug smile on his face. I didn't know what to do. I thought about calling the police and reporting him as a conman. But I didn't want to ruin the event by having the police come in. I was in the restroom, wondering what on earth I could do. I was just so . . . It's not like me to be clueless."

Callie almost had to laugh, as this was certainly true.

Iphy asked, "Do you have any idea how long you were there?"

"I stayed there for a while, thinking, and then I decided I just had to face Mrs. Finster and tell her the truth. But when I went to look for her, she was in the concert. I checked my watch, and I thought that maybe, as the concert had started soon after the argument I had had with Mr. King, he might not have gotten to her yet, and I could be first. So I sat in the concert myself and waited. But after it ended, she had to talk to all the people who had performed, and then word was out already about a dead body." Mrs. Forrester sighed. She looked bone weary. "I couldn't believe it. I just knew there would be trouble. I had no idea then that it had been done with *my* scissors."

She sat up. "Of course my fingerprints are on those scissors. I brought them and used them to cut some paper and tape for last-minute adjustments to the mystery book packages and to a sign pointing to our part of the event. But I didn't stab that man. I would never take a life."

Iphy nodded. "I believe you." She leaned over. "But you have to tell this to the police. Everything you've just told us."

"Also about the vase?" Mrs. Forester asked with wide eyes. "They will certainly see it as a motive on my part."

"You have to be totally honest. Then Falk can make the right assessment of the situation and help you."

"Help me? Lock me up, you mean. We all know he's not the sheriff. How I wish that man hadn't hit his stupid head on that beam over New Year's." Mrs. Forrester huffed. "He has thirty years of experience on the job."

Callie said, "Falk is doing great when the sheriff isn't around. He solved two murders earlier. You can rely on him to look at all the evidence."

With a sob Mrs. Forrester looked at her. "Easy for you to say—you aren't under suspicion. Falk wouldn't ever think you could be involved, since you're dating him."

Callie felt her cheeks heat at this remark, which sounded almost like an accusation. As if the idea of them dating was a crime in itself. "We're just friends."

It came out quickly, and she wondered for a moment why she was so eager to deny it was anything more. They were dating. Period.

But Ace made such a point of going to other towns on dates, avoiding them being seen together. Did he not see their relationship quite like she did? Would she look silly if it turned out she had expected too much?

Iphy said, "Falk is a very honest and hardworking man, Frederica. You know that. You just have to entrust yourself to his judgment."

Rubbing her hands, Mrs. Forrester huffed. "Did I hide out here in this dilapidated shack, cold and lonely, for nothing? I called you because I believed you would help me."

"How? By hiding you from the police? The fact that you ran and didn't give a statement has only made it worse." Iphy shook her head at Mrs. Forrester. "I will help you. I will do anything I can to clear your name. But I can't help you as long as you're making your own case worse by running from the police. You have to turn yourself in."

"Then they'll lock me up."

"Not necessarily. You can explain to them about the scissors and the argument you had with the victim. You can assure them you won't leave town. I can't see Falk throwing you in the cell. You're not exactly young anymore."

Mrs. Forrester harrumphed, but she also nodded slowly. "I see what you mean. I can't run forever. I didn't even mean to run. I just wanted to avoid being arrested in front of everyone present."

"That's understandable," Iphy assured her. "Now just come with us to the police station and tell Falk you want to make a statement of your own accord. Tell him you never meant to run away but just needed time to calm yourself. He knows normal people aren't used to murder cases. He'll understand it got you worked up, and you did a foolish thing."

Mrs. Forrester sighed.

Callie bet she didn't like to admit she had done a foolish thing. Even though today was different from any normal day. Frederica Forrester just didn't make mistakes.

Iphy patted her shoulder. "Come now. It's cold here. There's coffee at the police station. You can wash up a bit and have a hot drink, and then you can tell Falk the whole story. I'm sure he will lend a sympathetic ear."

"If I really have to." Mrs. Forrester rose to her feet, shoulders slumped.

Iphy said, "We all know you, Frederica. You're a determined woman who knows her own abilities. You'll overcome this trouble. Especially as you have friends who will support you through it."

Mrs. Forrester looked up. Suddenly she smiled. "You came for us back then. We were so afraid, you know. When it got dark and the rain lashed against the windows. Especially Billy. He'd never admit it, but he was so scared. He was almost crying. We all thought we were stuck here for the night. But you came. You didn't even scold us or yell at us. You just took us home and gave us hot chocolate."

Iphy smiled back at her. "Maybe the police station will have hot chocolate as well."

Chapter Seven

At the police station, it was quiet as one might expect on a normal evening in a small town. Callie walked in ahead of Iphy and a reluctant Mrs. Forrester, and caught sight of Falk standing at a colleague's desk, half leaned over, looking at the monitor of the computer the colleague was working on. The concentration in his expression, the slight tension in his posture, the way he supported his suntanned hand on the edge of the desk—it all etched itself into her memory right away, and she felt a smile creep up.

Ace just loved his job. It was his life, his identity, maybe even the way he was wired. Right now he was completely engrossed in whatever problem was unfolding on that computer screen, and he didn't even notice that some locals had walked in—that, in fact, the solution to one of his problems had walked in. He could now cancel that APB on the unfortunate library volunteer.

Callie cleared her throat, and Ace looked up. His expression changed for a moment when he saw her, warmth lighting his eyes, but then he discerned Mrs. Forrester behind her and immediately suspicion flashed across his features. He came to the counter and said, "Good evening. What's this? A committee?"

Callie sensed he figured that they were there to plead for Mrs. Forrester's innocence, and didn't like it. Annoyance formed in the back of her head that he hadn't even let them explain why they were there, but was instead ready to jump to conclusions.

Iphy said, "Mrs. Forrester is very sorry she ran off, Deputy. But she was in shock. In fact, she's still not feeling very well."

Ace studied the woman a moment and then said, "I can see that. Would you like some coffee?"

"With lots of sugar," Iphy enthused, putting an arm around Mrs. Forrester and leading her to the plastic chairs where visitors to the station could sit to wait for their turn to file charges or give a statement.

Ace made a gesture as if he wanted to stop them—Callie bet that the visitors' corner wasn't the place where he wanted to put Mrs. Forrester right now—but then he stopped himself, shook his head a moment, and went to fetch coffee.

He came back carrying four steaming mugs on a tray. Iphy had sat down beside Mrs. Forrester, and Callie and Ace joined them. Ace passed around the coffee and then sat quietly, waiting for Mrs. Forrester to speak.

Callie suspected he was burning with curiosity over where Mrs. Forrester had been, how she had ended up with Iphy and Callie, and what had really happened between her and the victim that afternoon at Haywood Hall, but he didn't pose a single question. Callie admired him for his psychological insight, sensing these moments were essential to settle Mrs. Forrester and get her to open up. Not in an interrogation room, where she might felt cornered, but simply here, sitting down over coffee like acquaintances meeting.

"I'm so sorry, Deputy," Mrs. Forrester said at last. Her face crinkled as if she was close to fresh tears. "I should have come up to you the moment you arrived. I was a coward." She hung her head.

"I can imagine you were shocked and didn't even believe it was really happening. But you're here now, and you came of your own accord. We can talk about it." Ace sipped his coffee.

Visibly relieved, Mrs. Forrester nodded. "I didn't kill him. You must believe me. I did handle the scissors and I did argue with him because he wanted to go back on his given word." She began to explain how the victim had suddenly asked for payment for his participation in the Valentine's event, and not just cash, but a vase from the house that wasn't hers to give. How he had even threatened her with a fake email he claimed to be able to produce to prove to Mrs. Finster the vase had been promised and had to be handed over to him.

Ace listened with a deep frown over his eyes.

Callie studied him, his broad shoulders, the gleaming star on his shirt, the changes in his expression as he heard the story and formed questions to ask later. She realized just how much she loved being a part of what he did. But it seemed that the closer they got, the more distant Ace became where his work was concerned, not wanting to involve her in anything he was busy with.

At least, it felt that way sometimes. Mrs. Forrester sighed and clutched her coffee mug. "I can't believe that he actually threatened me to play along with him. That he could produce an email in which I had allegedly agreed to pass something from the house to him. I don't understand technology well enough to know if it's possible to make such an email. He would have to have made it— forged it—as I certainly never sent it to him. I would never do a thing like that."

Ace sat up, leaning his mug on his knee. "Mrs. Forrester, I hate to say this, but your story is hard to accept."

Although Callie had expected some resistance on Ace's part—after all, it was his task to question people and see if their statements held water—she cringed under this judgment.

Ace continued, "This man had just had his big break on TV, and he was building a reputation as an expert in his field. Would he resort to such low tactics as putting pressure on a small-town librarian to give him antiques by way of payment for an hour's work? It seems unlikely."

Mrs. Forrester glared at him. "Well, it is what happened." She nodded firmly. "Why would I make it up?"

"You might have had a personal reason to fight with him, and you don't want to disclose this reason to us."

Mrs. Forrester tilted her head. "So this whole story I just told you is a fabrication? I tell you, if I had planned to invent a story, I would have chosen a better one. I had enough time for it!" Mrs. Forrester looked angry enough to get to her feet and storm off, and Iphy put a placating hand on her arm.

"That is true. Frederica had enough time to think things over while she was at the cannery."

"Cannery?" Ace asked, puzzled.

Mrs. Forrester snorted. "I know hiding places around Heart's Harbor you've never heard of, young man. I came here to speak with you of my own accord. Else you would have spent some time looking for me."

Callie was worried a moment Ace would get mad at the woman's tone, but she saw his brown eyes twinkle as if her feistiness amused him. "I'm just trying to explain to you that your story might seem unbelievable and make your position in this case very difficult," he said. "Your prints are on the weapon, and you argued with the victim shortly before he died. I don't see who else might have had a reason."

"There were so many people there," Mrs. Forrester objected. "This man had been on TV, and we advertised his presence there. Someone might have come over especially to see him."

"And kill him with a pair of scissors that were conveniently at hand and marked with a local person's fingerprints, to divert suspicion to someone else?" Ace sounded incredulous. He shook his head, got up, and went to refill his coffee mug.

"He does have a point," Iphy said with a worried expression. "If someone came in from the outside, not knowing Haywood Hall and how the event was set up, where the expert might be and that a weapon would be at hand, how could he or she have planned the murder? That just doesn't make sense."

"Maybe someone came to confront the expert about something," Callie suggested, "and the altercation got out of hand. The scissors were lying there, put aside after being used, and the killer grabbed them and struck out. It need not have been premeditated."

"True." Iphy nodded. "That does sound better."

Ace was just on his way back over to them when the phone rang, and the other deputy answered. He listened a moment and then waved at Ace. "A deputy from a nearby town thinks he saw Mrs. Forrester. She's having pancakes in the local diner. With an unknown man. He thinks the guy might be an accomplice to the murder. Should he arrest them both?"

Callie bit her lip in an attempt not to start laughing.

Ace flushed. "No, Mrs. Forrester is right here." He pointed at the woman. The other deputy, who apparently didn't know her, looked surprised, then puzzled. "But we have an APB out for her, right?"

"Yes, cancel that," Ace said, waving a hand. "And please let those people eat their pancakes in peace."

Callie didn't dare look at Iphy for fear they'd both burst out laughing.

Ace came back to them with long strides. He sat down and said, "No more APB, Mrs. Forrester, but you are still in a tight spot."

"Iphy just had a great idea," Mrs. Forrester said, and Iphy explained her suggestion for how the murder could have occurred without premeditation.

Ace listened patiently, but Callie just saw him mentally shaking his head at them.

When Iphy was done, Ace said, "To accept that an outsider murdered our victim, I have to have motive for the murder. Like I just said, this was a well-respected man."

"But not a pleasant man," Mrs. Forrester objected. "He was curt and condescending, and he outright yelled at his poor assistant."

"Yes," Callie said, "did you manage to talk to him? Could he perhaps tell you something about threats against his employer? Altercations he might have had over something he appraised?" She was thinking up options off the top of her head, but it could be possible. Especially if he had been a man with a temper like Mrs. Forrester suggested, he might have made enemies.

Ace said, "The assistant was very upset by the murder and just about passed out. The local doctor had a look at him and gave him a sedative to calm him down; then one of my colleagues drove him to his hotel so he could rest up before giving a statement. The doctor told me that pressing someone under shock to make a statement right away can distort his memory of the event and lead to unintentional lies. So I will have to speak to him later, once he has slept a bit and can think clearly."

Iphy glanced at Callie, and she had the impression her great-aunt had an idea. But Iphy didn't say anything.

Ace looked at Mrs. Forrester. "I'll have to take a formal statement. We don't need to do it in the interrogation room, but in the sheriff's office. What do you say?" Mrs. Forrester nodded. "I'm telling the truth, so I'm happy to make it formal, sign it and all." She waited a moment and then asked in a small voice, "I can go home after that, can't I? I don't need to spend the night here?"

Iphy said, "Of course not. There's no need to lock a woman your age in a cell. The deputy will understand that you're not running away."

Ace said, "But that's exactly what she did earlier today." Mrs. Forrester sighed and sat with slumped shoulders.

Ace looked her over. Then he glanced at Callie. Callie made a "come on" gesture with both her hands.

Ace sighed. "After you make your statement, you can go home, provided you promise to stay around Heart's Harbor. No more 'I panicked and I took off to think about it,' or you will be locked up. Understand?"

"Perfectly," Mrs. Forrester said, something of her primness returning as she rose to her feet and marched to the door of the sheriff's office. "Shall we, then?"

Ace rolled his eyes at Callie, but she did detect a hint of a smile. He was a good man at heart, who didn't want to put an elderly lady in jail. Thing was, to keep Mrs. Forrester out of further trouble, there had to be another suspect to offer to the police. Someone who might have wanted to kill the presumptuous book appraiser.

Iphy took Callie's arm and called after Ace, "Good night, Deputy. Thanks so much for seeing us. Always a pleasure to talk to you." and she dragged Callie along to the door.

Callie felt distinctly like Iphy was up to something, and Ace also seemed to sense it as he stared after them with narrowed eyes.

Outside, Iphy said in a low whisper, "That assistant must know more about people who didn't like the victim. We have to talk to him." She walked to the car. "The Cliff Hotel it is."

Callie rushed after her. "You can't do that. Ace hasn't even had a chance to talk to him. He's entitled to the first statement. You just heard how worried he is that the statement might get perverted and could contain unintentional lies. That assistant has to sleep off his shock and then talk to Ace."

"What I'm after isn't a statement about the murder," Iphy corrected. "Just some factual information so we can hunt down other suspects. We can't keep Mrs. Forrester out of trouble just by smiling at Ace Falk." Iphy gave Callie a look from under her lashes. "Not even you."

Callie flushed at what felt like a bit of a jibe, even when coming from her own great-aunt.

Iphy hopped into the car, buckled up, and reached to turn the ignition on.

Callie scooted in beside her, sighing, "Ace won't be happy about this. I don't want to risk a fight with him."

Iphy glanced at her. "All couples fight sometimes."

"Yes, but I don't want him to feel that I'm hampering him in his job. It means the world to him."

"You mean it might mean more to him than you do?"

Callie clenched her jaw. "I wouldn't have put it quite like that."

Iphy laughed softly. "Don't worry, darling. If you don't want to come into the hotel to speak to the assistant, I'll do it alone. You can tell Ace you didn't agree with me and told me so, but that I did it anyway because I'm a stubborn old woman who made a promise to help Mrs. Forrester."

Callie exhaled. "It's not going to make much difference to him whether I was actually there or not. Just the fact that you got to the assistant before he could . . ."

Iphy glanced at her as she steered the car through the dark night. "If it doesn't make much of a difference, you might as well come along. Two see more than one. I'm curious about the young man's feelings. Judging by what Mrs. Forrester told us, he was bullied by his boss. Why would he faint upon hearing the man was dead?"

"Well, not liking your boss isn't the same as wishing him dead," Callie objected. "We all know people who are a bit much, and wish them away sometimes, but then to find out he actually died—stabbed too— that is kind of gruesome. Maybe this assistant is a sensitive type?"

Iphy nodded. "Who knows? We'll find out soon enough."

Chapter Eight

The Cliff Hotel was a beautiful Art Deco building with revolving doors, behind which porters in red uniforms waited to carry people's luggage, direct them to the elevators, or answer queries. The man who stopped them as they came in, a tall individual with a big black moustache, looked doubtful when Iphy asked about the assistant of Mr. King.

"If you do not know his room number," he said in a weighty tone, "we are not allowed to give it to you. Privacy and all that."

"But it's very urgent," Iphy said. "Can we talk to the receptionist?"

"She will tell you the same thing," the man said with a suspicious frown, but he did allow them to walk on to the reception desk. A brisk young woman with blonde hair and impeccable makeup was clicking away at a keyboard and glanced up with a pearly smile when she spotted them. "Good night. How may I help you?"

"We're looking for the assistant of Mr. King. He was unwell this afternoon and was brought back here by the doctor."

Callie noticed that Iphy said "doctor," and not "police," although Ace had told them that one of his colleagues had driven the assistant to his hotel to rest up.

Iphy said, "We were just interested to hear how he's doing now."

"I assume he's fine," the young woman said. "I haven't heard of a doctor coming over since my shift started at seven PM."

So she wasn't there when the deputy had brought in the assistant, and probably has no idea about events at Haywood Hall either, Callie mused.

Iphy said, "We do have to speak with him if that's possible. Could you call up to his room and ask him if he can see us?"

The receptionist looked doubtful. "If he was unwell, he's probably asleep now."

"I understand, but someone died, and we really do have to talk to him."

"Oh." The receptionist looked startled. "That changes things of course. I'll call up to his room right away." She picked up the receiver of a sleek black telephone with one hand while clicking through screens with the other, apparently looking for the phone number of the room in question. She pressed some buttons and listened.

The phone seemed to ring endlessly. Just as Callie was certain no one was going to answer, the receptionist said,

"Hello, front desk. There are some people here to see you concerning a death. I see. But they say it's urgent."

She listened a moment. "I'm sending them up." She put down the receiver and smiled weakly. "The third floor. Room 332."

Iphy thanked her and rushed off to the staircase. Callie followed, a bit perplexed.

"I don't want to wait for the elevator, where that moustache man might come over to tell us we have no real business here," Iphy hissed to Callie. "Quickly—up the stairs."

Callie followed her energetic great-aunt, trying to keep her breathing steady as they pushed up two flights of stairs. Still, she was panting as they stopped in front of the door with the brass numbers 332. There was no one else in the corridor, which was carpeted in thick blue and had some nice oil paintings and watercolors on the walls.

Iphy raised a hand to knock, but the door was already open. A young man with tousled hair and a pale face peered at them. He wore checkered flannel pajamas and had his feet stuck into neat dark blue slippers. His expression turned from worried to puzzled. "I expected the police," he said.

Iphy smiled. "We're not the police, just some friendly locals who wanted to ask how you're doing now. Do you mind if we come in? It's so awkward standing in the corridor like this."

"Not at all—come in," the young man said. He stepped back and let them into the room. It was a large one with a double bed. On one side the duvet was folded back as if he had crawled out after he had gotten the phone call. Callie noticed, though, that the sheet covering the mattress was crisp, not crinkled.

There was an aroma in the air she couldn't quite place. Something sweet. Glancing around her, she looked for flowers that might produce the scent, but didn't see anything.

The young man gestured to a sitting area in the corner. "Please sit down. Do I know you? Yes, I remember seeing you at the event this afternoon, but I don't think we were formally introduced." He laughed suddenly, low and hoarse. "That's what my boss would have said. Formally introduced. He liked to sound smart."

"My condolences on your boss's death," Iphy said, seating herself in one of the leather chairs. "You must have been shocked."

"Well, it's not like I expected him to die so soon." The young man sat down on the end of the bed and reached up to rake his hand through his hair, making it stand up even more. "But I did know lots of people didn't like him. Someone had even warned him not to come here."

"Not to come here?" Callie echoed.

"Yes, he got a threatening note. Saying Heart's Harbor would bring him bad luck or something. He found it in the mail, laughed at it, and threw it to me. I read it as well and asked him if he shouldn't take it seriously. 'And do what?' he replied. 'Not go there? I accepted the invitation and I am going.' That was it for him."

"Do you still have that note?" Iphy asked, glancing at Callie. Callie was thinking the same thing: such a note could prove that the victim had been targeted before he arrived. It didn't clear Mrs. Forrester per se, as one could even argue that she might have been the one to send the note, but it could broaden the circle of suspicion.

The young man had gotten up and rummaged through a briefcase. He opened a beige file folder and pulled out a note. "I keep all of them."

"All of them?" Iphy asked, looking up at him as he moved closer.

"Yes. Since his debut on TV last Christmas, he gets lots of letters, threatening him or inviting him for the weirdest things. Even offers of marriage."

Iphy grimaced and shook her head as the young man wanted to hand the note to her. "We shouldn't get fingerprints all over it. Maybe the police can still lift some?"

The young man looked down at the note in his hand. "Of course. I'll put it back at once. I can give the entire file folder to the police. If you think it will help."

"I think it certainly might," Iphy said. "And so could your statement of what happened this afternoon. As soon as you're up to it, you must speak with the police."

"I was just so very groggy from this sedative the doctor gave me," the young man said. "By the way, how impolite of me. I still haven't told you my name." He reached out to Callie. "Seth Delacorte."

"Callie Aspen, and this is my great-aunt Iphy. We run a tearoom in town and help preserve Haywood Hall."

"Such a great house." Genuine appreciation lit Delacorte's eyes. "I could have wandered around all afternoon.

Not that I . . ." He lowered his head, flushing. "I did peek into a few rooms, just to see what was in there."

"But of course." Iphy smiled at him. "We open up the house for events so people can enjoy the rooms and decorations. I'm glad you had a look around. In fact, should you have to stay here for a few more days as the police investigate the murder, I would love to show you around."

Delacorte smiled and relaxed a bit. "That would be nice. Thanks." He looked from Iphy to Callie and back. "Why exactly are you here?"

Iphy sighed. "The death of your boss caused a stir. One of our local people was . . . well, not arrested, but it came close to that. She's suspected of being involved with the murder, but we seriously doubt that she could be."

"People aren't always what you believe them to be," Delacorte said. He had seated himself on the bed again, kicked off his slippers, and shuffled his bare feet. He looked eighteen, and Callie wondered how the puffed-up expert had chosen this shy college student to become his aide.

Iphy said, "We just want to help find out what happened."

Callie threw her great-aunt a warning look. Now that they knew there had been a threat against King before he even came to Heart's Harbor, and Delacorte possessed a file full of such threats that he would hand over to the police as soon as he got the opportunity, their job was done. Iphy had said in the car that she wouldn't ask about the murder and risk influencing his statement before Ace had gotten a chance to talk to him.

Delacorte leaned back, putting his hands on the bed. He seemed to weigh his words. "My boss was a very unpleasant man who managed to get into fights with people wherever he went. He made demands, and he went back on his word."

Iphy glanced at Callie as if to say that this conformed what Mrs. Forrester had told them. Callie wanted to signal her not to push it any further, but didn't know quite how, and Delacorte was already continuing to speak.

"Whenever we went somewhere and the atmosphere was pleasant and relaxed, I knew it wouldn't stay that way. I tried to avoid being nearby when the bad weather broke, but since I was his assistant, that wasn't easy."

He laughed softly. "It didn't matter to him whether I was there or not. You'd think he would behave better when other people were present, but maybe he didn't even see me as a person with an opinion. In any case, my opinion of him didn't matter." He scoffed.

Callie felt sorry for him as he sat there, pale and undone, feeling his way around a situation that was too big to grasp. She herself couldn't really believe there had been a violent death again and that she was a part of it.

"This time it was even worse." Delacorte fidgeted with a loose thread on the duvet. "He didn't just argue with the person who had invited him here, and say he was no longer working for free, but he also—"

Iphy raised a hand and interrupted him. "You overheard the argument with Mrs. Forrester?" The excitement in her expression betrayed that her thoughts were racing. She was assuming Delacorte could confirm to the police that his employer had told Mrs. Forrester he wanted to be recompensed for his efforts and that he'd even asked for a vase from the house, claiming Mrs. Forrester had previously promised it to him.

Delacorte shook his head. "The argument started in my presence, but then he drew her aside, and I couldn't overhear any details. I just know he was at it again, breaking his word. I wanted to leave the house and not come back. But I work for him, so I couldn't really leave."

Callie said, "You were just saying Mrs. Forrester wasn't the only one he argued with."

"That's right." Delacorte tore the thread off the duvet and held it in his hand, glancing sheepishly at it. Then he dropped it to the floor and sat up. "He also fought with that singer. They almost came to blows."

"Singer?" Callie echoed, glancing at Iphy.

Her great-aunt sat in her chair, clutching the armrests as if to gain a firmer grasp.

"You mean the baritone invited to join the orchestra?" Callie asked.

"Yes. I saw them. That singer was holding my boss by the shoulders, shaking him."

Callie cringed at the mental picture conjured up. Once Ace heard about this, he would see another suspect all right, but not one that would be more agreeable to Iphy than Mrs. Forrester had been.

"But that's not logical at all," Iphy protested. "Sean didn't know he was coming here. He took the place of someone else at the last minute."

Callie nodded. "That's true. Our engaged singer, Simon Teak, got a throat infection, and Mr. Strong agreed on short notice to cover for him. He flew in especially from Vienna."

Delacorte shrugged. "I don't know about that. But I did see them struggle. I will have to tell the police."

"Of course, but . . . uh . . ." Iphy clapped her hands together and nervously knotted her fingers. "Could you overhear what it was about?"

"No. Like I said, I liked to stay far away from his fights with people. I didn't want anything to do with it." Delacorte pulled up his legs and hugged his knees. He looked even more pale now.

"Perhaps you should get back into bed," Callie suggested. "You don't look well. You should tell all of this to the police. I'm sure it will really help Mrs. Forrester's case."

And, she added to herself, *get Sean Strong into trouble. Something that seems to upset Iphy quite a bit.*

Delacorte nodded at her. "I'll talk to them when they contact me." He leaned his chin on his knees. "Anything else?" He sounded quite weary.

"No, we're leaving." Callie rose to her feet. "Thanks so much for seeing us at this inconvenient moment. Could you give me your phone number in case I have another question?"

"Of course." Delacorte got up, walked to the closet, and extracted something from the pocket of the suit that was hanging there. He handed her a card. "Call me any time."

Callie nodded. "Thanks." She gestured to Iphy. "Good night, and thanks once more for seeing us." As she stood beside the low table, waiting for Iphy to rise, her gaze brushed across the table's surface and noticed a bit of wetness there, a half circle like that formed by a glass that has a drop of something along the bottom. There was no glass in sight, though.

"Good night then." Delacorte let them out the door. They heard him lock it as they walked away across the thick carpet, which muffled their footfalls.

Iphy stared ahead with wide eyes.

Callie put a hand on her arm. "Sean Strong," she said. "What can it mean?"

Iphy looked at her. "I don't know. But I have a bad feeling about it. Sean is an impulsive man."

Callie's heart sank. "You mentioned that last time he was here, things went wrong. Did he fight with someone? Is he violent?"

Iphy didn't say anything.

Callie pressed, "If you know something, you have to tell Falk. He'll find out about it eventually, I suppose, and he'll be mad when he discovers that you knew about this prior incident and kept it from him."

"It was such a long time ago, does it really matter? Can it be related?" Iphy seemed to talk more to herself than to Callie. "I wonder. I don't want to think that of him, but . . . Oh!" She wrung her hands. "Why does this have to be so hard?"

Callie stopped her at the elevators. "What's hard?"

Iphy eyed her, shadows under her normally laughing eyes. "Seeing him again. Meeting up again and realizing what you dreamt of, hoped for." She smiled ruefully. "I would have sworn before today that it was all over and done with. Too long ago to matter. Too long ago to bring any more hurt. But now . . ." She fell silent and stared into the distance, her posture tight and still.

Callie said, "You have to tell Falk what you know. He'll decide what to do about it."

Iphy came to life and looked at her. "No," she said, determinedly. "I'm not going to Falk just yet. I want to talk to Sean first. If I read him right, he'll be staying here, at this hotel. This is just the place for him. Let's go find out."

Chapter Nine

The woman at the reception desk eyed them with suspicion when they came up again. "Didn't you manage to speak with the gentleman in 332?" she asked, her neatly plucked brows drawing together.

Iphy nodded. "We did speak with him, but we also have to talk to someone else who's staying here. Mr. Sean Strong."

"About this same death?" the receptionist asked in a doubtful tone.

Suspecting trouble—and possible eviction from the hotel—Callie hurried to say, "The death happened at an event, and several people are involved. That is, they knew the victim and have to be informed of what happened."

"Don't the police usually do that?"

Callie smiled. "Mr. Strong is aware of the death. He just needs to know about some related issues. He performed at our event, so we do want to speak with him."

"And you do not have his cell phone number?"

Iphy put her hand on Callie's arm. "Let's just leave," she said in a weary tone. "I'll have to go look up his cell phone number. Although I don't see what harm there is in simply calling the gentleman's room to inform him that we're here."

The receptionist sighed. "Oh, well, I suppose I can do that. Your name was Callie Aspen?"

"And Iphigeneia Aspen," Iphy added with emphasis, as if that name would make all the difference.

Callie wondered if it would.

"One moment, please." The receptionist checked her records on-screen and picked up the receiver. "Two ladies are at the desk for you. Callie and Iphigeneia Aspen. They say it's about the event you performed at this afternoon. Yes? Very well." She lowered the receiver. "He's coming down in a moment."

Callie noticed that Sean Strong didn't ask them to come up to his hotel room, but perhaps if he knew Iphy from some prior occasion that hadn't ended well, this made sense.

Maybe they should be glad he wanted to talk to them at all?

It took a few minutes before the elevator bell dinged and Sean Strong appeared. He was dressed more casually than he had been that afternoon, in a purple cashmere sweater and gray pants. He walked over slowly, his eyes on Iphy. "So we meet again," he said and then leaned over to peck her on the cheek. Callie could smell a fresh, invigorating, piney aftershave. As if he had put it on moments ago.

She studied her great-aunt's reaction with interest.

Iphy looked up at Sean Strong, her expression undone and vulnerable. "Have you spoken to the police about the murder?" she asked softly.

Strong nodded. "Of course. They wanted statements from everyone. Not that there was much of a point to mine. I was with the orchestra the entire time."

"Not quite," Callie said. "I ran into you outside, remember? Shortly before it began. You asked me for coffee, and I brought you into the drawing room."

Strong looked her over as if he wondering why she had brought that up. "Does it matter?"

Callie took a deep breath before adding. "People also saw you arguing with the victim."

Strong hitched a brow at her. "And how would you know that? Are you with the police?"

Before Callie could respond, he said to Iphy, "A grand-niece with the police now?"

Callie wondered if Sean Strong had committed a crime in Heart's Harbor and had left in disgrace. She could easily picture him as a charming cat burglar.

Or a swindler taking single ladies' money with fancy promises he never made good on?

She shivered a moment at the idea that Iphy had fallen in with a crook who had left her heartbroken.

"Callie is not with the police, Sean; she's helping me at Book Tea these days."

Strong smiled softly. "Ah, Book Tea. So that's still your life."

"Yes, more durable than some other things."

He winced, lines tightening around his mouth. Then he gestured at the arched entrance to the hotel bar. "Shall we have a drink?"

Without waiting for their reply, he walked to the archway.

Iphy shot Callie a quick look and then followed. Callie wasn't quite sure what she had seen in her great-aunt's eyes: alarm, uncertainty, or even a hint of excitement? Was she still under the spell of this dashing man?

Callie rushed to catch up with her and watch it all play out.

Strong was at the bar, ordering something. Then he came over to them and directed them to a table in the far corner. There was nobody around to overhear them. He waited until Iphy had taken a seat and then gave the chair a polite little push into place. Callie noticed he touched Iphy's shoulder a moment. He didn't do the same with her when he stood behind her chair. Callie smiled up at him. "Thank you. I hope you aren't too annoyed with the situation?"

Strong took a seat and looked at her, confused, it seemed. "The situation?"

"Well, a fellow singer asks you to step in for him; you graciously agree to do so, flying out all the way from Vienna; and suddenly you're embroiled in a murder case?"

"Oh, that." He said it as though it was but a minor thing—an hour's delay at the airport. "Like I just said, I have nothing to do with it."

"Callie may not be with the police," Iphy said, playing with her bracelet, "but she is seeing a police officer. Deputy Falk, who is leading this case."

Callie flushed at the ambiguous word *seeing,* which left the question open of how serious their relationship really was. Ace had been so reticent to be seen with her.

"And?" Strong studied her with a half frown.

Iphy shrugged. "I'd be careful about lying."

"I'm not lying. I was with the orchestra."

"But not the entire time," Callie said. "Or else you couldn't have been observed arguing with the victim."

"Our source claims," Iphy added, "that you were holding the victim by the shoulders, shaking him. That suggests more than just a few exchanged words in passing."

Strong leaned back. "I have no idea what you're talking about."

Iphy shook her head. "The source will speak with the police and be considered reliable. He was close to the victim. He—"

"He may be lying to shift suspicion."

A waiter brought drinks. A whiskey for Strong and a raspberry mocktail for Iphy. Strong gestured to Callie. "The young lady still has to order."

After Callie asked for mineral water and the waiter left, Strong lifted his whiskey glass and toasted Iphy. "To the old days."

Iphy seemed reluctant to touch her glass to his. "What did you fight about with the victim, Sean?"

Before he could repeat that he had no idea what she was talking about, Iphy continued, "We both know you're a determined man when it comes to something you feel deeply about."

Strong leaned over to her. "I was asked to step in and do this performance. Yesterday around this time, I was still in Vienna, going about my business. Do you really believe I came to an event and then got into an argument with an unknown man and killed him?"

Iphy held his gaze. "You tell me." She waited a moment and then said, "If someone had told me you'd come to Heart's Harbor, I would have put money against it."

"Is it so hard to believe I would do a fellow singer a favor?" Strong shook his head. "You have a dismal view of me."

"I think you might have done someone a favor, but not when hearing it involved coming here." Iphy kept her gaze on him. "Why, Sean? I don't understand."

He gestured with both hands. "I just wanted to help out. And it was all so long ago. Does it really still matter?"

"Of course not." Iphy sat up straighter. She reached for the raspberry mocktail and toasted Strong, jutting her chin as if in a silent challenge. "To the old days, then."

Callie watched her great-aunt take a sip while never taking her eyes off the man.

Strong seemed confused by the sudden change in her. "Now you accept my arrival without question?" he asked.

"If you say so." Iphy sounded light, almost teasing. But her expression became serious again as she lowered the glass and said, "You did tell us the truth about the murder, didn't you, Sean? You're not involved?"

"Of course I'm not involved. I'd never even heard of that guy." Strong made a dismissive hand gesture. "He might be a big name here because he's been on TV, but you don't hear much about such things across the pond. I spend so much time in Europe, I consider myself more European than American these days."

Iphy nodded. "I suspected you'd feel that way. You've always been a man of the world."

"And what are you then? A small-town girl?" He leaned over and shook his head, his dark eyes lighting. "You can't make me believe it, Iphy. Your talent is wasted here. You could have worked at patisseries all over the world. Vienna, Paris, Rome, Sydney. They would have been fighting to engage you."

"And everywhere I would have been the worker—never the owner, never the boss. Book Tea is mine, Sean, to do with whatever I want. I have freedom to make my own creations, not churn out what others decide for me." Iphy studied him. "You should have understood that was most important to me."

"Freedom?" he asked, with a strange little smile. "Oh, I did understand that."

There was a long, tense silence. Strong nursed his whiskey; Iphy tore apart the mint leaves on her mocktail. Callie had the strong impression that both of them were back in another scene, another meeting, a long time ago, replaying events in their minds, maybe wondering if it might have been different if they had acted in another way, had spoken other words.

Strong said, looking at Callie, "So you're seeing a police officer? The guy who was on the scene this afternoon? What was his name? Hawk?"

"Falk," Callie corrected.

"Oh yes. It reminded me of Falco, falcons. One bird or another." Strong gestured. "I was never an outdoor person. Did you grow up here? Have you always craved to work in the tearoom and live this small-town life?" His question sounded challenging, almost disparaging.

Callie sat up. "Not at all. I was a tour guide. I've been to all those cities you just mentioned and then some. Budapest, Warsaw, Moscow, Venice. I've seen the northern lights and stood in the Parthenon. Explored catacombs and palaces."

He smiled appreciatively. "Sounds like an exciting life. Still, now you're here. Did you get sick perhaps and couldn't travel anymore?"

Callie shook her head. "It wasn't a decision made for me by circumstance. I made a conscious choice to change my life around. To settle here in Heart's Harbor."

"Settle?" Strong said it as if it was a dirty word. "I see. For love perhaps, for the deputy?"

"I . . ." Callie paused a moment, as her attraction to Falk *had* been part of her decision to settle down, the idea that she should get serious about finding someone to spend her life with, maybe have a family with. She wasn't as young as she used to be.

But here she was, living close to Ace for months already, and she still didn't know for sure what he felt for her. Yes, there was an attraction; yes, they were dating, having a good time together, but they rarely had a deep conversation about anything. Ace often looked so tired from his work that she wanted their dates to be about relaxation only, having fun.

But they never really talked about their pasts, their values, their ideas for the future. Was their connection serious enough for a real relationship? Did she even want that?

Strong held her gaze. "You sure take a long time to answer. There's no shame in it, I suppose. People like to settle. Most of them." He glanced at Iphy. "There are just a few rolling stones who don't want to gather moss."

"I hope you've been happy," Iphy said.

"Happy?" Strong scoffed. "What is happiness anyway? I've traveled. I've performed at some of the most spectacular places in the world. Music makes me happy, a near perfect performance, a night where everything comes together."

Callie noticed how Iphy shrank a moment under the latter words. Had there been a night, back then, when Iphy had believed everything would come together for this man and her? Their attitude toward each other now was far too charged to assume they had known each other only superficially.

Strong emptied his glass and gestured for the waiter to refill it.

"You shouldn't drink too much before bed," Iphy said.

Strong smiled at her. "It helps me sleep. Better than pills, I suppose." He leaned his elbows on the table. "Now what exactly did you want to talk to me about?"

The waiter came with a new glass and took away the old. Iphy waited until he had retreated before saying, "I want to know what you argued about with the man who was murdered this afternoon."

"I told you, we didn't argue. Your source lied."

Strong looked confident as he spoke. Still his hand tightened on the whiskey glass, and he gulped down the contents in a few drafts. He put the glass on the table with a thud. "If that's all, I'm off to bed. I'll be flying back to Vienna tomorrow."

Iphy shook her head. "You can't leave. You are part of —"

He rose to his feet. "I gave a statement. I have nothing to do with it. I'm leaving. Goodbye." And he turned on his heel and marched off.

"What a strange man," Callie observed. "When he came from the elevator, he seemed almost glad to see you. I had a feeling he had even dressed up for the encounter." She studied her great-aunt from aside. "He was very attentive, getting you your favorite drink and being so gallant with the chairs. Now he's just walking out on us?"

Iphy sat motionless, staring at the spot where Strong had vanished from sight. "Something is wrong here," she said. "I can't imagine that Seth Delacorte lied to us about having seen Sean with the victim, shaking him. Why would he make that up?"

Callie shrugged. "Strong said it might have been to divert suspicion."

"But Delacorte would know we would ask about it, or the police will if he tells Falk the same story. So why risk it? He could have said someone argued with the victim, shaking him, not naming the person, claiming he only saw him from behind and didn't know him."

Callie sipped her mineral water. "He doesn't want to confide in us. We can't force him to."

Iphy sighed. "I should not have told him you were seeing Falk. That must have spooked him."

"Why, if he has nothing to hide?" Callie leaned over. "Has he been involved with the police before?"

Iphy stared at her. "Why on earth would you think that?"

"Well, it was obvious this afternoon that you were rather shocked to see him here. I just thought he might have run some con here in the past."

Iphy held her head back and laughed. "Sean, a charming conman. I admit the role would be perfect for him. His tongue is so glib." Her laughter died, and she stared into the distance again.

Callie touched her arm. "I'm sorry he came here. Bad luck he was asked to take Teak's place."

Iphy sighed. "Yes, him of all people. But I guess I should see the bright side of it. I once told myself that if Sean ever came back into my life, I would feel I had made the wrong decision back then."

"And what are you feeling now?" Callie asked.

Iphy looked at her with a hint of alarm in her eyes. She looked at the raspberry mocktail and suddenly got to her feet. "It's getting awfully late, and we do have to work tomorrow. Come along."

She went to the bar to pay for the drinks, but the waiter said the gentleman had told him to put anything they ordered on his hotel bill. Iphy seemed to doubt whether she could just accept this offer, but Callie touched her arm and nodded toward the exit. They left and gave the receptionist, who still seemed wary of them, a friendly greeting.

Outside, Callie breathed the chill February air with relief and said, “That’s that then. We did all we could.”

Iphy nodded. “I just hope Sean isn’t serious about leaving. I don’t think Falk will appreciate it.”

Callie studied her closely. “You’re worried that Delacorte told us the truth about Strong shaking the victim in a fierce argument.”

Iphy’s eyes were sad. “Yes, I’m almost certain that Sean lied to us. And I don’t know why. I just hope that . . .” She wrapped her arms around her shoulders a moment.

Callie studied her with wide eyes. “Are you afraid he could be the murderer?”

Iphy shrugged. “I don’t know what I’m afraid of. But I have a bad feeling about this whole thing. Him coming back here and . . .” She pressed a hand to her forehead. Then she looked up and forced a wan smile. “Let’s go home and get a good night’s sleep. Maybe I’ll feel differently in the morning.”

Chapter Ten

Callie remembered those words first thing when she woke up the next morning. A vague worry about her great-aunt's state of mind niggled at her, and she got out of bed quickly. She greeted Daisy and went to shower and dress. Then she made Daisy some breakfast but decided to drink only a cup of coffee herself, with a few rice crackers, and then drive out to Book Tea right away to go see how Iphy was. She could have a better breakfast there. First of all, it was nicer having breakfast with someone than all on her own, and second, Iphy made the best pancakes Callie had ever had.

She had just arrived at Book Tea, Daisy in her basket in the passenger seat beside her, when a police car came from the other direction. The two cars pulled up simultaneously, turned into empty parking spots. Callie put the brakes on and got out. She waved at Falk. "Ace! Good morning."

Ace gave her a less than enthusiastic wave back. He came over and said, "Someone should make a law against early morning arrests. They drain all the energy I need for the rest of the day."

"Poor you." Callie rubbed her hand down his shoulder. "Come on inside for a bit of breakfast. I'm here to enjoy Iphy's fabulous pancakes, and I'm sure she can make a few extra for you."

Ace's face cleared. "That would be great."

Callie took him and Daisy around to the Book Tea's back entrance and knocked on the back door before pushing it open and stepping in. Callie inhaled, expecting the invigorating scent of coffee and eggs, or toast, or pancakes, but there didn't seem to be anything on the air at all.

As she came into the kitchen, she found it empty, the sink pristine, with no traces of cut-up oranges or some spilled coffee, and her great-aunt was nowhere in sight.

Ace hitched a brow at her. "Where can she be? Still in bed?" He checked his watch.

Callie shook her head. "The back door was open, so she must be up and about. She locks it overnight."

"A wise precaution, even in a small town," Ace said. "Do you want to go see where she is?"

"Yes." Callie told Daisy to stay with Ace, and with an uneasy feeling in her stomach, she rushed upstairs. She knocked on her great-aunt's bedroom door and got a groggy reply. She opened the door an inch and peeked in. "Hello. Good morning. Are you not feeling well?"

"I couldn't sleep." Iphy replied from under a heap of blankets. "I must have fallen asleep in the early hours, and now I feel like I got no sleep at all."

"You stay in bed. I'll fix you some breakfast."

"Just tea and toast. I can't eat anything substantial right now."

"Okay." Callie closed the door again softly and rushed downstairs.

"She just didn't sleep very well." Callie tried to sound light. She didn't want to attract Ace's attention to the fact that something upsetting might have happened the previous night. She felt bad enough knowing where she had been and what she had done. "A nice chance to treat her, instead of the other way around." Callie turned on the tap to fill the kettle with water for tea.

"Can I help you?" Ace asked. "I do great omelets."

Callie nodded. "Sure. The frying pan is in there. Eggs and butter in the fridge."

Ace opened the fridge, with Daisy standing beside him, looking up as if she expected him to produce some ham or other treat for her.

"Just ignore that," Callie said.

Ace came back to her with eggs and butter, and put them on the counter. He collected the pan and hummed as he went. Callie suddenly wondered what it would be like to live under the same roof with him and make breakfast together like this every day.

As if he would have time for that, she scolded herself. *He's always off to work early.*

Ace buttered the pan and put it on the stove, then beat the eggs in a bowl. While Callie made toast for Iphy, the scent of omelets began to fill the kitchen.

"On toast?" she asked Ace, and when he nodded, she also put bread in the toaster for the two of them. She ran up with Iphy's tea and toast, and when she came back in, Ace had already put plates on the table, and the toast was ready to eat. They sat down opposite each other, with hot toast and fresh omelets, while coffee brewed in the maker.

"Pretty perfect," Ace said around a bite.

"Your omelets?" Callie asked with a grin.

"No, this moment." He smiled at her, a leisurely smile that warmed her inside.

She held his gaze, not minding that her food was getting cold. He was right: this was perfect. The perfect start to the day. She had done the absolute right thing coming back to Heart's Harbor and settling here. This was real life, not all the traveling about from one hotel to another, where breakfast was good, but also impersonal. Life was about forging bonds with special people.

Then Ace's phone rang, and he pulled it from his pocket to answer it.

Callie hoped he wouldn't have to rush off right away. She listened intently to his end of the conversation.

"Yes," he said. "Yes, I see. Okay. I'll do the interrogation when I get back. Just let him sit there and think it over. Yeah, right. Later."

He lowered the phone and looked at her. "Is that coffee about ready?"

"Sure." Callie got to her feet and filled two mugs, handing him his. As their fingers touched, Ace smiled at her again. She leaned over and kissed him on the lips. He tilted his head. "What's that for?"

"Just because I'm happy to see you."

He grinned. "Same here." He pulled her over to sit on his lap. She leaned her head against his, and they just sat there, listening to the vague sounds coming in from outside, a car in the distance, singing birds.

Then Ace said, "I can't stick around much longer."

"I know, just a minute or two." Callie wrapped her arms around his neck. "I see too little of you. You're always working."

"Yeah, well, maybe I can solve this murder quickly. Got a suspect in the interrogation room now who checks all the boxes."

Callie studied his excited expression. "Means, motive, opportunity?"

Ace nodded. "Means is easy. Those scissors were lying around for anyone to grab. Motive can be found in the argument the suspect had with the victim. And opportunity—"

The word *argument* made a little jerk pass through Callie's body. "Who did you arrest?" she asked with an unsettling feeling in her stomach.

"Sean Strong, the baritone."

Callie sat up. "Really? You established that he did fight with the victim?"

"The victim's assistant said so. I went to the hotel early to speak with Delacorte, and as soon as he mentioned Strong, I wanted to talk to him. He was staying at the same hotel, so

I expected this to be a matter of just knocking on his door and taking a statement. But it turned out he had already left for the airport." Ace tensed as he spoke. "I went after him with blaring sirens and caught him just as he was about to check in." Ace looked satisfied. "I took him back in cuffs. King's assistant said he was rather violent so you never know."

Callie stared at him. "But are you sure you're not—"

"Barking up the wrong tree? Definitely not. I just got that call." Ace patted his pocket where his phone was, his smile of satisfaction deepening. "My colleague told me that they checked with the guy this arrested baritone was supposed to replace—Teal or something."

"Teak," Callie corrected. "Simon Teak."

"Yeah, right. He doesn't have a throat infection at all. Strong told him it was super important to him to do this performance in Heart's Harbor. He even paid Teak the fee he would have gotten for it so he could take his place."

Callie's heart sank. Strong had come to Heart's Harbor on purpose. He had wanted to be at the event where the expert came to appraise books. He had pretended he didn't even know Mr. King, as the TV show he appeared on at Christmastime was virtually unknown in Europe, but apparently he had known him well enough to come out and . . . confront him?

Yes, their altercation hadn't been random either, two men colliding and telling each other, heatedly, to watch their step. No. A confrontation after he had consciously looked for it. For a chance to meet up and . . .

He had lied to them last night. Logically, of course, if he was guilty of murder.

Callie's chest tightened at the idea that Iphy's old flame was a murderer. How would she ever work through that? She was already sleeping badly.

"What's wrong?" Ace asked. His hand brushed her cheek. "You look so pensive."

"Thing is, Iphy knows Sean Strong from some prior occasion. She didn't tell me anything about it but I had the impression they were"—she didn't know exactly how to put it—"close at the time."

Ace stared at her. "The man I just arrested is a friend of Iphy's?"

"I —" Callie realized it might be better to tell him everything right now, but Ace cut her off with a hand gesture. "Better if I don't know." He gently pushed her off his lap. "I have to get going and question him. Just don't tell Iphy anything yet. You never know what reason he might have for coming out here. Could be something perfectly innocent." But his tone didn't support his words.

Before Callie could protest, however, or ask questions, Ace was at the back door. "Thanks for breakfast."

And he was gone.

* * *

Callie was reluctant to go up to Iphy to collect the tea mug and plate, as she was certain her perceptive great-aunt would notice something wrong right away. She hung around the kitchen, cleaning the breakfast items, and then went to walk Daisy.

Outside, in the pale sunshine of a crisp February morning, everything didn't seem so bleak. After all, Strong had assured them he'd had nothing to do with the murder. If he had told them the truth.

But why would he have told them the truth anyway? He was a virtual stranger. That he had known Iphy sometime in the past didn't mean anything now. If he was guilty, if he had killed that man in a moment's rage, grabbing for the scissors and stabbing them into his chest, he wasn't going to admit it to them. Iphy obviously wanted to help Strong, but would he be open to that? He seemed like a man who knew how to fend for himself.

No. Callie shook her head to herself. If Strong was the killer, he would have played the exact part he had played last night. He would have been friendly to them and accommodating, denying all involvement, hoping he could elude the police long enough to be on the plane back to Vienna, where he couldn't be arrested.

How clever. How cold-blooded, if he was truly guilty.

Callie could still see his pleasant smile as he had walked over from the elevator and pecked Iphy on the cheek. Ordering her favorite drink for her, toasting "the old days." Anything to be seen as charming. And harmless perhaps.

Though Callie doubted whether Iphy had ever felt like Sean Strong was harmless.

While Daisy frolicked on the grass of the little park, Callie stood staring into the distance, trying to determine how to best handle this. Her first impulse was to keep the arrest from Iphy and hope she wouldn't find out anytime soon. But as Book Tea was full of gossiping ladies, it might be hard to do that.

And as soon as Iphy learned about it and about the fact that Callie had known and not told her, she would be angry about it. Perhaps honesty was the best policy after all?

But Callie already knew that Iphy would want them to clear Sean. They'd have to go to the police station, where Ace would not be happy to see them. He had been so sweet to her this morning, so approachable, giving her new hope they could be together more and even have a life together? Why not?

But this murder case shouldn't ruin it. Ace hadn't liked her involvement in earlier cases because he was worried for her safety, and she didn't want to risk an argument with him.

Daisy came back to her and stood beside her, looking up as if she had noticed her pensive mood. She barked and wagged her tail.

Callie leaned down and cuddled her. "Thanks for trying to cheer me up, girl. We're going back home. I just wish I knew what to do."

Daisy trotted ahead of her at a brisk pace, not realizing what decision waited for Callie as soon as they were back at Book Tea. They found Iphy in the kitchen, fully dressed and making coffee. "Are you sure you didn't want to rest a bit longer?" Callie asked, realizing how convenient it would have been if Iphy had stayed away from Book Tea and the guests for the day.

Her great-aunt turned to them and smiled. "Thanks so much for bringing my breakfast to me, but I'm not ill. It's a normal day, and I intend to work hard." It sounded like something she had told herself a couple of times, maybe while trying to drag herself out of bed.

"You never take a day off," Callie said. "Maybe you should." She gestured to the back door. "Just go for coffee in another town. Walk by the ocean. Go see a museum. Do something that will be a pleasant diversion."

Iphy's eyes narrowed as she looked Callie over. "Is something the matter?"

"Why would something be the matter? I just realized you're always so busy, and you should take care of yourself. If you had a bad night, take some time off."

Iphy leaned her weight back and crossed her arms over her chest. "What's going on here? The moment I came into this kitchen, I smelled male aftershave."

She waited a moment and then asked, "Has Sean been here? Has he set up a plan with you to take me out for the day?"

She acted like she was disgruntled about it, but it didn't escape Callie how her great-aunt's eyes lit up at the idea. A whole day spent with the man she had once cared for.

Maybe still cared for?

Callie's heart sank. With the best intentions, she had wanted to send Iphy out for the day but had now inadvertently given her hope that Sean Strong wanted to spend time with her, when in fact he was at the police station, facing murder charges! How to break the truth to her in a gentle way?

"I know Sean probably pressed upon you to keep it a secret from me, lure me away from here with some excuse. But you can't lie, Callie. I see right through you." Iphy's eyes twinkled, and there was a bit of color in her cheeks now. "Just tell me. Then I'll also know what to wear."

She stood, ready to rush upstairs to change into other clothes, select jewelry, put on perfume.

Callie's chest tightened. Poor Iphy. She really didn't want to be the bearer of this bad news.

"You're not giving anything away by telling me what's up. I won't tell Sean you told me either. Now just confess."

Callie said, "Sean wasn't here. Ace was. We had breakfast together."

The elation in Iphy's features died. Her cheeks got even redder, though, as if she was embarrassed by her own hopeful assumptions. "Oh, well, I guess . . . yes, that is logical, of course."

She turned away to the coffeemaker and fussed with her mug she had put at the ready. She didn't seem to think anything of Ace's arrival in the early morning or think to ask whether he had mentioned developments in the murder case.

Good. Now she need not tell her great-aunt anything.

But looking at her narrow shoulders, Callie just couldn't keep the truth from her. She couldn't bear to go into this day waiting for the bad news to hit. Waiting for that person to step through the door and discuss the sensational arrest at the airport that Iphy would overhear. What if she dropped something, broke her precious china, drew attention to herself?

No, she had to tell her now.

"Ace told me he had made an arrest. At the airport."

Iphy turned to her. "Airport?" Her blue eyes were wide and alert. "You mean, the killer was trying to flee?"

"That's what Ace thinks. He arrested him, and while he was here with me, a call came in that they also found out the arrested person lied about certain things. That strengthens their case against him."

"Him. So it's a man. Mrs. Forrester is off the hook then. I never thought it was her." Iphy spoke fast, almost forced. "Did Ace . . . um . . . mention who it was he arrested?"

"Yes." Callie swallowed a moment. "Sean Strong."

Iphy blinked. It seemed she got the message at once but was furiously trying to deny it or twist it in some way to explain to herself that Sean had been arrested but wasn't guilty.

The high color drained from her face, and Callie rushed to put an arm around her and help her onto a chair.

Iphy said in a low voice, "Sean? No. That can't be right."

"He was arrested while he was trying to get on a plane"

"That flight back to Vienna had been booked in advance. He didn't try to run. Did you tell Ace that?"

"No, I didn't tell him we saw Sean last night."

Callie figured her great-aunt would understand why, but Iphy tried to pull away from her, saying, "Then he doesn't even know. I have to go and tell him."

Callie sucked in air. "Sean can tell Ace he was already booked on that flight. He can also explain to him why he lied. To Ace, to us, to everyone."

"Lied about what?" Iphy looked up at her, her eyes wide with shock and disbelief.

"He came to the Valentine's event to replace Teak, right? Simon Teak with his throat infection."

"Yes. It's impossible to sing with a throat infection."

"I know, but unfortunately Mr. Teak doesn't have a throat infection or any other ailment preventing him from performing yesterday. He is in perfectly good health and told the police when asked about it that Sean Strong offered him money to let him take his place."

"What?" Iphy stared at Callie.

"Sean Strong deliberately changed places with Teak so he would be at the event yesterday. Combine that with the knowledge that he fought with the victim, and we can conclude that he came here because he wanted to meet up with our expert, Mr. King. Confront him about something."

"That is so far-fetched," Iphy said. "Sean might have changed places because he wanted to come back to Heart's Harbor. He *has* been here before."

Callie shook her head. "Last night you said you would never have believed he'd come back here."

Iphy blinked. "Yes, well, I can be wrong sometimes." She laughed, a shrill little laugh. "He did want to come back."

Callie clenched her hand at the idea that Iphy now believed Sean had wanted to come back for her. That he had used an excuse so as not to let her know it had been his choice that had brought him there, rather than a coincidence or a favor for a friend from the music business.

"Sean was always a proud man," Iphy said softly. "He never liked to admit he had been wrong. Maybe he didn't want to admit he was wrong leaving this little town the way he did. Maybe he wanted to come back and make up. But he didn't want to say so in so many words, so he used the excuse of the throat infection as a reason why."

She looked up at Callie again, hopeful, eager. "That must be it. I'll go to the station and tell Falk. It's all a silly misunderstanding."

Callie shook her head. "Sean told us last night he had never heard of this expert. But he fought with him. Not just with words—he also assaulted him. Coincidence? I don't think so. If he came here for a purpose, the dead expert was that purpose."

"Nonsense." Iphy pushed herself up on the table's edge. "Why would Sean, who has a wonderful life in Europe, drop everything and come here to murder some man who appraises books? That makes no sense at all. I'll explain to Falk that Sean came here for old times' sake. Then he can let him go again."

"Ace won't just let him go," Callie protested, but her great-aunt had already rushed off to go get her coat.

Callie went after her. "You're in no condition to drive. You're tired and upset."

"I'm not . . ." Iphy turned to her with a wild gesture, almost losing her balance and falling against something. She smiled wanly. "All right then. No need to have an accident added to the list of disasters. You can drive me out to the station. But you won't interfere in it. I'll talk to Falk alone."

"Please do." Callie already felt bad about the whole thing, as she had a sinking feeling that Iphy's explanations wouldn't change Ace's mind. But she wasn't about to let her exhausted and upset great-aunt go alone. She slipped into her own coat and, with Daisy, they left the Book Tea in a rush.

Chapter Eleven

At the police station Callie was happy to see Ace wasn't in direct view, suggesting he might already be interrogating Sean Strong. She hoped she could avoid him—or at least avoid the impression she had shared her knowledge of the arrest with Iphy immediately after Ace had left her and that they were now here to interfere in the case.

Iphy went to the desk and asked for Deputy Falk. Callie hovered at the door while Daisy pressed against her leg. The dog seemed a bit intimidated by the loud sounds of keyboards clicking, faxes rattling, and phones ringing.

The deputy behind the desk gestured and called something, and to her annoyance, Callie saw Ace appear from the corridor leading to the interrogation rooms. He came over to the desk, spotting Iphy, and looked past her, seeing Callie. Callie wasn't quite sure what the words were for the expression on his face, but it came close to unpleasant surprise.

Irritation even.

Iphy explained something Callie couldn't hear, and Ace frowned, as if he wasn't about to comply. Then he relented and waved her along to an office that wasn't used. He closed the door behind them.

Callie felt nervous that he hadn't even acknowledged her with a nod or a wave of the hand, nor asked his colleague to offer her coffee while he was talking to Iphy.

She paced the floor where the sitting area was, too nervous to sit down and look at one of the dog-eared magazines about boating and fishing, littering the low table. Daisy walked beside her, her head tilted in confusion at what on earth they were doing there, but after a while she got tired of it and lay down, putting her head on her paws.

"You're right, girl," Callie said with a rueful sigh, "taking it easy is better, but—"

A sound behind her jerked through her, and she whirled around. But it was just an elderly woman entering the station. She stood a moment, looking around her, apparently insecure and perhaps even intimidated by the idea that she was now in a police station. Callie wondered briefly where she had seen her before, but as the Book Tea received countless visitors every day, she assumed it had been there and didn't pay much real attention. She resumed pacing, checking her watch and determining Iphy had already been in there for seven minutes. It seemed much longer.

Ace's colleague had gone to the desk to ask the new arrival how he might help her, and the lady started to explain in a quivering voice that she had been to Haywood Hall but had been told there that she had to come to the police station.

"Come here?" the deputy asked. "Do you know something about the murder that happened the other day?"

The woman looked startled. "Oh no. I know nothing about the murder. I had no idea that the man had died until they told me at Haywood Hall. I only want my book back. I will return the twenty dollars he gave me for it. I should never have brought it, let alone sold it. But my husband insisted."

Oh yes—now Callie remembered. The woman was one half of the elderly couple who had offered some book from a relative's inheritance to the book appraiser, and Mr. King had offered to buy it from them for twenty dollars. The woman hadn't actually wanted to part with the tome, but her husband had said that then at least a part of the useless inheritance would have delivered some value—or something like that. Callie felt a bit sorry for the woman, who had apparently been forced into the decision and had regretted it right away.

"I thought," the woman said, "that my book was maybe still at Haywood Hall, and I could get it back. I brought the money." She opened her right hand, showing a folded bill. "I just want it back."

The deputy still didn't seem to follow. "You left a book at Haywood Hall yesterday?" he queried with a puzzled look.

"No, the expert bought it from me. But I never meant to sell it." The woman bit her lip, her expression crinkling as if she was about to cry. "I only want it back."

Judging by the deputy's expression, he still didn't fully understand, and Callie walked up to the two of them and said, "Excuse me for overhearing your conversation. Perhaps I can help?"

The elderly lady nodded at her in grateful appreciation of the offer, and although the deputy seemed less pleased, Callie pushed on. "I organized the Valentine's event at Haywood Hall, and the expert was there to put a price on books and buy them if the owners were willing to part with them. But I understand you're not happy with having sold?"

The woman shook her head violently. "I never was. Bill forced me into it. He never liked Mother, and he just wants to get rid of her things, not caring what they're worth."

"I understand they may have emotional value to you," Callie said.

The deputy seemed relieved now that he didn't have to deal with the upset woman, and he let her talk.

"Real value as well," the old lady said with a prim little nod. "That book is worth more than twenty dollars—I know it."

Callie decided to let this layman's guess pass and asked, "Did they tell you at Haywood Hall that the book would be here?"

"Yes. Mrs. Keats told me that all the things the expert had handled had been taken along by the police. Including my book." She held out her hand again with the bill. "Here's what he gave me. You can have the money and let me have the book back."

The deputy shook his head. "We can't hand over something that's part of an ongoing investigation."

"But it's my book, and it had nothing to do with the murder."

The deputy said, "The book is staying right here." He straightened up a bit, leaning his hands on the edge of the reception desk. "Besides, if you sold it to this expert, technically it's his now and not yours anymore."

"But I want it back. He forced me into selling it. It's worth much more, I know."

The deputy looked at Callie, raising a brow as if to ask what he should make of this. "I will take your name and contact information, ma'am, and then Deputy Falk will get back to you about it later."

The old lady protested that she just wanted her book back and didn't see why he couldn't give it to her right now, but as he insisted she should provide her information, she did give in with a sigh as he wrote it down on a sticky note. She showed him the money two more times, claiming he had to give the book back to her on the spot, but then, as he wished her good morning and turned his back on her, she seemed to understand she wasn't getting anywhere and shuffled off, clutching the money in her fist.

As soon as she was out the door, the deputy said to Callie, "She should understand that once she sold it, it became his. There's nothing we can do about it. It's not like he stole it from her."

"She made a decision under the pressure of the moment and her husband's insistence. I don't see why she couldn't get her book back if she repays what he paid her."

"It just doesn't work that way," the deputy said, shaking his head as he put the sticky note on a desk in the back. "The dead man bought it from her fair and square. Just like an old lady to believe it was worth much more. It's probably just a worn book with mold on it."

Callie wanted to reply, but a door closed and Iphy appeared, walking ahead of Falk. She held her head high, and Callie sensed there had been an altercation of some sort, as Ace's expression was tight, his jaw clenching.

Iphy passed her without saying anything and went outside. Callie wanted to follow her to ask what on earth had happened, but Ace pointed a finger at her and said, "Miss Aspen, in the office a moment, please."

It sounded so formal that Callie feared for a moment she'd be arrested herself. Her heart skipped a beat, and she stood rooted to the ground. But then she tried to laugh off her own fear and followed Ace, with Daisy hard on her heels.

As soon as they were inside the office and Ace had closed the door, he turned to her and said, "What do you think you're doing? Your great-aunt wouldn't admit it right away, but the information she provided to me to clear Mr. Strong gave her away, and after I pointed that out to her, she couldn't deny it. You went to the Cliff Hotel together last night and have talked to witnesses and suspects."

"We didn't know then that Sean Strong was a suspect," Callie protested, but Ace ignored her and continued, "You went behind my back, talking to people I hadn't even had access to, like the victim's personal assistant, Delacorte. I don't understand." He stood a moment, inhaling and clenching his fists, as if he was controlling himself with only the utmost effort. "This morning I come to town, and you invite me to have pancakes with you. I tell you I arrested someone and there Iphy is, running over first thing to tell me how wrong I am to have done this and saying I should have investigated the threats against King instead."

Callie bit her lip. She could understand that Ace hated her great-aunt judging his actions, especially the arrest, which he considered justified based on the evidence available at the moment.

Ace continued, "I don't want a civilian coming in here telling me how to run my investigation. Besides, Iphy *knew* Strong planned on leaving town first thing this morning, and she didn't report to me last night to inform me of his intentions. He could have gotten away, leaving me empty-handed."

"His flight was booked in advance," Callie added in her great-aunt's defense. "He was only here for that one performance at the Valentine's event."

"That performance, huh? That's what Iphy tried to sell me too. That he wanted to perform here for old times' sake. Well, I bet you he came especially to meet that expert and he killed him."

Callie wanted to protest, but Ace cut her off with a hand gesture. "It ends here, Callie. I realize now how wrong I've been to share things from the investigation with you. I shouldn't have mentioned the arrest this morning. I was happy to see you and spoke to you when I shouldn't have."

Callie's throat tightened. They'd had breakfast together, felt at ease together, like a real couple, but now . . .

Ace said, "I don't want to say you used me to get the information, but you knew about Iphy's meeting with this man last night, and you agreed with her to keep his imminent departure a secret from me."

"I did no such thing. Like I said, his return flight had been booked in advance, and we even told him he couldn't leave town because he was also involved in the murder investigation. But he assured us that he had given an initial statement, and as he had nothing to do with the murder—"

"That's up to me to decide." Ace was white with anger now. "I let it go before because you were helping friends or even my sister, but I can't tolerate this anymore. You have to stop messing with my investigations."

"Messing? Like I ruined them or something? Two times I helped you catch a killer. I even risked my own safety for it. Doesn't that count?"

Ace said, "That's just it. Citizens shouldn't risk their safety—that's for the police to do. If something had happened . . ."

He was silent a moment, his expression tensing as if he was considering the consequences of Callie getting injured—or worse—during a confrontation with a killer.

Then he said, "This morning was the last time I will share something of an ongoing case with you. It was a grave mistake, and I regret it."

He hesitated as if he wanted to say more, then opened the door and said, "Goodbye."

Callie stared at him. Was he serious? He was just kicking her out? Out of the investigation, out of his police station?

Out of his life as well?

What did it mean?

Confused, she stood a moment, trying to find something to say to soften him, then decided this was the wrong moment, as he was just too angry, and she herself was also far from calm. She passed him without saying anything and left the station.

Outside, Iphy sat in the car, waiting for her. As Callie climbed in and strapped herself in, Iphy said, "Falk probably talked you into persuading me Sean could be guilty. But I don't want to hear it. Sean may be an impulsive man, but he's no killer."

Callie couldn't believe her ears. Here was her great-aunt immediately assuming she would listen to Ace and start to persuade her of Sean Strong's guilt, while moments ago Ace had accused her of siding with Iphy.

Her hands were trembling, but she forced herself to try to speak calmly. "I'm not trying to talk you into anything. It's none of my business. After all, you told me precious little. About the past or about what is happening now. And that's fine. But I don't want to be caught in the middle."

"Of course not. You don't want a fight with Falk. But he's doing the wrong thing, ignoring those threats and focusing on Sean only. He's letting the real killer get away. That certainly wouldn't be good for his career."

"Possibly, but Ace is no mood to listen to such reasoning now. He's livid about what we did last night. He doesn't seem to realize that I was against going to the Cliff Hotel in the first place."

Iphy sighed and knotted her fingers. "I meant to keep you out of it. Act like I had gone there alone. But when Falk started to cross-examine me—that's what it was, a cross-examination, as if I was under suspicion of murder myself!" Iphy's voice shook with suppressed indignation. "I slipped up and mentioned your name. Then he knew, of course."

Callie drew a deep breath. Iphy didn't want to hear a defense of Ace right now, and frankly, Callie didn't even know if she wanted to defend him. He had just blatantly accused her of conspiring with Iphy. And he had said he didn't want to see her anymore. That was what he had said, right?

More or less.

How could he?

After all they had been through together.

But together didn't mean anything to him. It was always about work. His work, his badge, his reputation. "Miss Aspen" he had even called her in front of the other deputy. He had always taken her to other towns on dates, as if to hide their relationship. Like it was a guilty secret, something to be ashamed of.

Well, after today he wouldn't need to be ashamed anymore.

She clenched her hands and leaned back hard in the car seat. Like she needed him.

Iphy said, in a forced tone as if she was controlling herself with difficulty, "I'm sorry for involving you. I shouldn't have done that."

Looking at her great-aunt's pale face and tight jaw, Callie wanted to reach out and ask her to tell her what exactly had happened in the past between her and Sean Strong, throwing her off balance now. But it seemed unlikely Iphy would want to confide in her at that moment. Better to let the emotions calm down a bit and talk then.

Iphy drove back into town without speaking to her again. At Book Tea she vanished into the kitchen, where two of her helpers were already baking and asking her why she hadn't been there. Iphy didn't answer their questions, but simply took the pink fondant rolled out on the counter and started to decorate cupcakes, which were the weekly special.

The helpers exchanged astounded looks but then turned to their own chores, one cutting a goose shape from gingerbread dough. Once baked, it would be decorated with white frosting and a blue jelly bean to represent the blue carbuncle found inside it in the famous Sherlock Holmes tale. The other helper was cutting out letters. The idea to form your own names or messages of love had been a great success at the event, and they had decided to make it a part of the tearoom's offering as well.

Callie watched the bustle a moment and decided she wasn't needed there. She was just about to leave when someone asked where Peggy was, as it was her shift too.

"I'll go see where she is," Callie offered at once, eager to get away from the charged atmosphere. She walked the stretch from the Book Tea to Peggy's house, going so fast that Daisy could barely keep up with her. Anger surged in her veins, and she just wanted to kick something. How could Ace treat her like that? Of course he hadn't been happy that Iphy showed up, pleading for Sean Strong, or that he had found out through his cross-examination, as Iphy had called it, that both Iphy and Callie had been to the Cliff Hotel last night to speak with Strong. As if they would give sensitive information to a potential killer.

Callie sighed as her anger retreated to make way for regret and worry. She didn't know if Sean Strong was a killer. She did know Iphy was sort of under his influence, and if he was somehow caught up in crime, that could be very dangerous. She should have told Ace about the bond between Iphy and Sean right away that morning, when he had revealed the arrest to her. She had, of course, mentioned that Iphy knew Sean from before, but Ace obviously had no idea this meant Iphy was willing to take risks for him. And Callie had wanted to explain a bit more, but there had been so little time.

Callie halted and rubbed her forehead. She had handled part of it wrong, even without realizing that in the moment. To protect Iphy, she should have involved Ace from the beginning, instead of keeping him at arm's length. Of course, Ace had been angry when Iphy had been forced to reveal everything, and not in a neutral way, but to defend someone Ace had just locked up. What a mess.

And aside from them having had contact with Sean Strong last night, which she might have been able to explain as contact between old friends meeting up again, they had also talked to Seth Delacorte, the dead man's assistant. There was no excuse for that. It had been wrong. Ace had let the guy go back to his hotel to sleep off his shock, and before he had managed to take a statement they had talked to him. What had they even been thinking? Helping Mrs. Forrester, sure, but . . .

It was a poor excuse. Callie only had to put herself in Ace's position to know she had been wrong and it must have been very irritating for him.

No. Not just irritating. Even potentially disastrous for his career. People knew they were dating. Even with Ace's precautions of not advertising their relationship, there were locals who knew. Or at least suspected and gossiped about it. If she then appeared in places talking to witnesses, as he had put it, it looked odd. It could get him in trouble.

Why had she done it?

She bit her lip. She should have apologized right away instead of acting like she still supported her decision to do it. Then Ace wouldn't have been so mad and told her to leave.

He'd told her to leave.

It was all over.

After all, could he turn her out of the station like that but still appreciate her company privately?

Callie sighed, and Daisy pushed herself against her leg with a low whine. Callie lifted the Boston terrier in her arms and cuddled her. "I don't know how I'm going to solve this, girl. But let's find Peggy first."

At Peggy's house she went around back and found Peggy in the kitchen, on the floor, surrounded by a ton of reusable food storage containers. There was a stack of lids lying to her left side, which she was trying to match to the bowls. Apparently, she had thrown herself into some early spring-cleaning.

As Peggy noticed Callie at the back door, she jumped to her feet and checked her watch. Her cheeks flushed. "I'm sorry it got so late. I'll get my things and come right with you." She rushed off and reappeared soon after in her coat and carrying her bag.

They locked up and left. Peggy didn't say much as she walked beside Callie, her collar turned up against the breeze, which still had a winter's bite.

"You could have called," she offered at last.

"I wanted a walk." Callie took a deep breath. "The murder is on my mind."

"I see." Peggy seemed to perk up now that it was about something other than her complicated relationship with Quinn. "Can I help?"

"I don't think so. Ace really doesn't like us snooping around."

"We don't need to snoop around. Just listen well to all the gossip at Book Tea. Didn't you tell me that before, after the murder this summer?" Peggy nodded with a satisfied smile. "I could use something to take my mind off things." She rushed to add, "Have you heard any more about why someone would want the man dead?"

"Just that he was rude to people, pushy, and self-centered. That usually means people hurt others and create enemies. But for someone to kill him, it must have been pretty bad." Callie tried to adopt a light tone. "There were people, for instance, who didn't like the price the appraiser had offered for their wares. But would they kill for that?"

Peggy shrugged. "Maybe if they felt cheated in a big way."

"There was a lady this morning who wanted her book back." Callie told it as if the incident had played out at

Haywood Hall, not wanting to reveal to Peggy that she had been to the station that morning with Iphy. She figured it was better to keep her great-aunt's former entanglement with the suspected baritone under wraps.

Her head hurt thinking of all the things she had to keep a secret from this person and that. Why did everything have to be so complicated?

Peggy said, "Well, you can decide to part with something and then regret it. I hope she can get her book back."

Callie nodded, not really listening or caring. A group of women flocked to Book Tea, having just come off a tour bus. They were chatting busily, pointing out shops down the street to one another, apparently intending to go shopping after they'd had tea.

Peggy said, "We'd better get busy. And keep our eyes and ears open."

Callie hemmed. "I think Ace can handle this one on his own."

Peggy gave her a startled look. "You do?"

Callie shrugged it off and was happy to step into Book Tea's warmth and buzz of voices. It would be good to be busy for a while and not think of all the trouble they had ended up in.

Chapter Twelve

At lunchtime Quinn came into Book Tea. Callie recognized his tall posture and blond head right away, and her breath caught as she wondered how Peggy would respond to his arrival. She kept her eyes on Peggy's face as she took an order and then turned away from the table, scanning the crowd for new arrivals who might also want to be served. As she saw Quinn near the entrance, she froze and stared at him with a vulnerable expression on her face, then turned and rushed into the kitchen. Quinn narrowed his eyes a moment, as if he was undecided, then pushed forward and followed her.

Callie didn't think a confrontation would help, especially not in the kitchen where the other helpers were at work, and headed to intercept him. She tapped him on the shoulder. "Hi, Quinn. Can I help you?"

"I want to talk to Peggy."

"Right now might not be the best time."

"I've been calling her since yesterday, but she isn't answering the phone." Quinn's breath rasped. "I want to talk to her. Explain. Ask her to come to lunch with me."

Callie took a deep breath.

"Please?" Quinn said.

Callie wanted to say no, then realized that as long as Peggy avoided answering the phone and Quinn didn't stop calling, nothing would be solved. "All right, I'll ask her. But I can't guarantee she'll say yes."

"Of course not—just ask her. It would mean the world to me if we could just talk it over."

Callie felt uncomfortable under Quinn's pleading gaze, as she had a sinking feeling Peggy wouldn't want to go to lunch with him. With a heavy heart, she walked into the kitchen. Peggy was filling cups and putting muffins on plates. There was no one else there, which might not last long, so Callie said quickly, "Quinn wants to know if you want to go to lunch with him."

"So you're Quinn's mouthpiece now?" Peggy sounded harassed.

"I'm just conveying a message. I don't think he'll leave unless you say something. Go to lunch with him, or promise you'll answer his calls later today, or . . . something, anything."

"You have no idea what this is like, and you're telling me what to do?" Peggy looked her over with flashing eyes.

"I'm just trying to—"

"Yes, everyone is trying, but I'm the one with the—" Peggy burst into tears and ran out through the back door.

Callie followed her. Outside, she caught sight of Peggy, who had run smack into Ace. He held her by the shoulders and asked what on earth was wrong. Peggy said something, pushed past him, and vanished. Ace looked at Callie. His expression was puzzled, then turned cold. "Peggy doesn't need you to tell her how to run her life."

"Oh, really?" Callie said.

"She just told me you want her to do something she doesn't want to do."

"Great. Run to your big brother and complain. Last time someone I knew did that, we were in kindergarten." Callie turned away and went back inside. She slammed the door in his face.

She was certain he would leave, and her heart beat fast as she realized she didn't even know why he had come. Had he wanted to talk about that morning? Listen to her explanation maybe? Why was she yelling at him now? Ruining everything? Before she could slap herself, however, Ace opened the door and came in. He looked around the kitchen, making sure they were alone, and then said, "I need to talk to Iphy. I want her to hear it from me and not via the grapevine."

Callie's heart rate sped up even more. "Is it bad news?"

"It's for her to decide if she wants to tell you or not."

Oh yes, of course. Iphy could just decide not to tell her, and then she would be cut off completely. Everyone blaming her for something she couldn't help either! That Quinn had expressed his feelings for Peggy, that someone had died . . . "Fine, I'll go get her."

Iphy was just saying goodbye to some regulars, accompanying them to the door and waving them off. When she turned, Callie waved to attract her attention, and Iphy came over at once.

Callie said, "Falk is in the kitchen. He wants to tell you some news. I can't be there, and you have to decide if you want to tell me what it is." As she walked away to take an order, a hand landed on her arm, and she found Quinn beside her, asking what Peggy had said.

Callie had to refocus a moment to remember what he was talking about. Oh yes, Peggy and his request for her to go to lunch with him. "She doesn't want to come right now. It might be better to try and talk to her later."

Quinn said, "Did you tell her how important this is to me?"

"I didn't get much of a chance."

"But I need someone to plead my case. Callie, please."

Callie felt like her head was about to burst. They all wanted something, and she genuinely did want to help them, but it was just getting her into more and more trouble, and she was done with it.

"If Peggy doesn't want to talk to you right now, that's her choice. Following her around isn't making it any better."

Quinn seemed to accept her words, hanging his head and nodding. But as Callie turned away to take the order, at last, he suddenly made a dash for the kitchen.

No!

Leaving the startled customers, Callie darted after him and just witnessed him barging into the kitchen saying, "Peggy, I never meant to make you cry, but—"

Ace straightened up from where he had been leaning against the sink, his expression becoming suddenly alert and watchful. Callie would rather have run off than see what happened next, but she wasn't fast enough. "*You* made Peggy cry? I knew you were no good from the moment I laid eyes on you. I should never have let you near her or the boys."

Quinn looked around the kitchen, confused. "Where's Peggy?"

"She left," Callie said.

Ace looked at her, comprehension lighting in his eyes. "You wanted her to do something she didn't want to do. You put pressure on her to listen to this guy's lousy excuses."

"No," Callie and Quinn said in unison, but Ace didn't listen at all.

He stood there, gesturing wildly. "Just leave her alone, okay?" Ace made a move toward the back door, when Quinn said, "If she left to be alone, she doesn't want to see you either."

It was silent in the kitchen for a few moments, during which time Callie felt like everything was in slow motion. Like you see something sliding and falling to the floor, but you can't catch it in time, and you're already waiting for the bang as it shatters and the shards go everywhere. She was certain Ace would jump at Quinn and grab and shake him, and tell him he was the last person who had the right to say something like that.

But Ace didn't jump or do anything. He just watched them as if he was letting it all sink in, and then he said in a cold, remote voice, as if he were an answering machine, "I was giving Iphy some information she needs to hear. Could you both please leave?"

Quinn took a deep breath like he was gearing up for an argument, when Callie grabbed his arm and hissed, "Leave!" and ushered him out of the kitchen. She was glad Ace hadn't done anything rash, but she wasn't so sure that deep down inside he hadn't decided on something rash anyway, just something that didn't immediately show itself in his actions.

"I want to talk to Peggy," Quinn said. "She just misunderstood. If she needs more time, I'll give it to her. I never meant to hurt her. Honestly, Callie." He stood there, staring down into her eyes, apparently oblivious to the fact that they were now back in the tearoom, and people were casting them curious looks.

Callie said in a whisper, "Go—and don't contact Peggy right now. I'll call you later, and we'll talk about it. Promise. Just don't make it any worse."

"He'll do that for me," Quinn said, pointing at the door into the kitchen. "I bet he told her I'm no good for her and the boys. He just said as much."

Callie shook her head. "Ace just misunderstood. He doesn't know what you said to Peggy that made her cry. He probably thinks she's serious about you, and you're not about her."

"Of course you have to defend him. After all, he is your boyfriend." Quinn sounded almost disgusted. "I'm leaving. And don't call me. What for? I'll figure this out myself."

Callie stood there, completely deflated. First Iphy had accused her of being Ace's mouthpiece; now Quinn thought the same of her. Peggy believed she was advocating for Quinn, while Ace thought . . .

Callie raised a hand to her head. She couldn't take it anymore. But with Peggy gone and Iphy detained in the kitchen to hear Ace's news, she couldn't just leave. There was a tearoom to run here. She forced a smile and walked to the table where the customers were still waiting to have their order taken. "Things are a bit hectic," she explained. "Have you made your choice?"

Chapter Thirteen

After the rush of lunchtime customers was over, Callie had a moment to go find Iphy. Her great-aunt was putting the final touches on a fairytale cake for a young customer that would be picked up later that afternoon. Tiny roses decorated the castle where Sleeping Beauty rested on a bed of marzipan, her frosted hair streaming down the bed to the floor, where a cute little dog also lay snoozing. *Almost too pretty to eat,* Callie concluded absentmindedly, as she watched her great-aunt's busy hands putting a marzipan flag on the castle's tallest tower. It was pink with a tiny gold crown decoration. Iphy always worked out the smallest details to perfection.

Callie's throat constricted at the idea of how much she loved Iphy and Book Tea and what they had together, and how sad it was that they had argued about someone who had been away from Iphy's life for so long. What was it about Sean Strong that had immediately engaged Iphy again?

Callie said softly, "Ace said you don't need to tell me what his news was, and I'm fine with that, really. But I just want to know if you're all right."

Iphy glanced at her. "Fine." She took her time attaching one more tiny rose to the castle wall and then said, "As if Falk would keep anything from you."

"Oh, believe me, he would." Callie got a mug and filled it with coffee. Iphy didn't speak. Callie was certain she would just ignore her and finish the cake, but then Iphy came to stand beside her. "Falk didn't tell you?"

"He didn't even hint at what it was." Callie sipped and winced as the hot coffee hit her tongue and palate.

Iphy asked, "Did you argue about this thing with Quinn and Peggy? I have no idea what happened, but it seems they fought, and everyone is upset about it. It sounded like Falk—"

Callie raised a hand. The whole explosive situation was still fresh on her mind, and she didn't need her great-aunt to rehash it and bring up the emotions again. She also wanted to resist the temptation to tell Iphy that the friction with Ace had started because of Iphy's insistence they get involved with the murder case. But she wanted to get her great-aunt to open up to her about her past with Sean Strong, and blaming her now would not help that. "Let's not talk about what Ace does and doesn't do. I just want you to know I'm here for you if you want to talk. This whole thing with Sean Strong . . . I'm worried for you."

"For me?" Iphy snorted. She grabbed a tea towel to rub some reddish marzipan leftovers off her fingers. "I can manage."

Callie sighed. "Fine." She blew into her coffee.

Iphy said, "I do need your help, of course, to get him off the hook."

"Which hook?"

"The murder accusation." Iphy eyed her as if she wondered what Callie had been thinking. "My past with Sean is one thing, this whole murder business another. He's accused, and it sounds serious."

Callie looked doubtful. "We shouldn't get involved. We have no idea why he really came here."

"That's just it." Iphy looked dejected. "I fear Sean came here for me, and now the police interpret it as if he came to kill someone."

Callie focused on her coffee for a few moments and then said, "Sorry, Iphy, I don't want to hurt your feelings, but it seems highly unlikely that a man who came here for a simple reason like visiting an old friend wouldn't simply tell that to the police if it can clear him of suspicion. At least of the suspicion of having looked for a chance to meet with the murder victim and kill him."

"I know, but it's all so painful. Sean is a gentleman; he didn't want to get me involved in it."

"You already *are* involved in it. You went to the station to plead for Sean."

"But he doesn't know that, I suppose. Why would Falk have told him that?" Iphy fidgeted with a tea towel. "Sean just doesn't want word of the whole thing getting around."

"To protect your good name or his own?" Callie tilted her head, trying to understand how everything fit together.

"How much do you know? I suppose Achilles never mentioned it."

Callie blinked. "You mean Grandfather?" Achilles Aspen, Iphy's brother, was a fond memory from Callie's childhood, when she had visited his house and looked at his amazing book collection and played with the tin soldiers he had collected. Although he had died before Callie had turned eight, she still remembered those afternoons with a warm feeling inside. "What does Grandfather have to do with Sean Strong?"

Iphy sighed and folded the tea towel in half, then quarters.

Suddenly Callie understood why she had been so reluctant to share about the past. It involved more people than just her and Sean Strong, people Callie knew and cared for. Her heart sank at the idea that she would learn anything here which would change her opinion of her dear, book-loving grandfather. For if his role in all of it had been innocent, Iphy wouldn't have needed to keep it from her.

"I set up Book Tea with money I borrowed from Achilles." Iphy's voice was soft and wistful. "In those times, it wasn't as common as it is nowadays for a woman to start a business on her own, and my parents were traditional, not open to the idea at all. But Achilles believed in me. In lending me the money, he went against our father's wishes, which was something momentous. I loved Achilles for it, but I also felt indebted to him. Not just to repay the money as soon as I could, but also to make him proud, show him I deserved his faith in me. and that he hadn't alienated Father for nothing. Then I met Sean."

Iphy stared ahead, lost in memories. "It was the start of the summer season, tourists were flocking in, and this handsome man appeared in my tearoom, complimenting me on my coffee, saying it was better than what he'd had all over the world. He told me about Paris and Vienna and places I had only read about and dreamed of. He asked me to have dinner with him sometime, and eager to hear more about all the cities he had been to, I agreed. After dinner we walked by the ocean. He bought me ice cream at a little stand, and . . ."

Iphy's expression was tender. "It was so easy to fall in love. It would have been perfect, I suppose, if he had lived nearby. If we could have seen more of each other, gotten engaged in due time, and then married. But Sean had engagements in Europe. He was leaving again soon. He asked me to come with him. He said that someone as talented as I was would find work soon enough in a patisserie."

Callie recalled Strong referring to this when they had sat with him in the Cliff Hotel's bar. "You didn't want to come along because you would be an employee elsewhere, and here Book Tea was yours," she paraphrased her great-aunt's words.

"That's what I said to Sean, recently and in the past. But my real reason was Achilles. I didn't want to let him down by leaving. Father would never have stopped telling Achilles how he had made me all wild, lending me money and getting ideas into my head, eventually leading me to throw all caution to the wind and run off with a man. Father and Mother would have blamed Achilles for my choice, and as the eldest son, he would have been mortified."

Iphy smoothed the tea towel. "Family meant so much to me. How could I risk it all for something silly like being in love? I knew Sean so little, I—yes, it felt like we were meant to be together, and I longed to just go away with him, but . . ."

She smiled sadly. "I didn't dare take the chance. He had bought tickets for Vienna, you know, for both of us. He told me to pack my things and meet him at the harbor around eight PM, and from there we would leave for the airport. My heart clenched at the idea of leaving Heart's Harbor, Book Tea, of ruining Achilles' faith in me, and . . . I didn't tell Sean I wasn't coming when we kissed goodbye that day. I was too much of a coward for that. I couldn't bear to see the disappointment in his expression or face his questions. I asked him once how his family felt about his traveling, and he told me they were barely in touch, so I knew the concept of family didn't mean the same to him as it did to me. I went home and considered everything, and I didn't go to the meeting at the harbor. Around eight thirty, Sean came to Book Tea and knocked on the door, and I pretended not to be there. I was on my bed, crying."

Iphy blinked. Her eyes seemed to be full of tears as she recalled it. "I let him down, believing it was for the best. Falling in love and rushing off to Europe was just silly, nothing for a clever businesswoman like I was. I was afraid of people's opinion of me, about Achilles' opinion, my parents', and deep down inside, I was also afraid Sean's feelings would pass quickly, and he would leave me all alone in a strange country where I knew no one. That I would have to come back home in shame."

"That's understandable." Callie leaned over to her in comfort.

Iphy sniffed. "Is it? I told myself so a thousand times over the years when every now and then Sean Strong came back to mind. How he had smiled at me, how his eyes had lit up when I walked up to him, and how warm his arm was around my waist as we walked by the ocean. I had made the right decision, I reiterated—I had, because now I had beautiful memories, untainted by what might have been next: his feelings fading, fights, betrayal. It was better this way. But when I saw him again, Callie, I realized it wasn't better this way. I should have taken chances. I should have tried. Maybe it would have ended in disappointment, but at least I would have tried." She hung her head, and tears dripped down her cheeks.

Callie bit her lip. She could understand her great-aunt's rational decision at the time, but also her doubts now as she told herself that it could have been different. Her own head was full of questions about Ace and her, their chances for a relationship, her disappointment that he could be so cold, and at the same time the realization that she was a part of the problem, as she had gone against his express wishes, making him feel like she didn't care for his opinion at all. But things were never that straightforward.

"Anyway . . ." Iphy dabbed impatiently at her tear-stained cheeks. "I feel like I let Sean down in the past, and I won't do that again. I realize he's just a stranger now, as so much time has passed, but I can't sit by and let him be accused of murder. Maybe he did trade places with Teak on purpose," Iphy said, gesturing with her hands. "And the medical examiner found marks on the dead body suggesting a violent struggle took place just before King died, but that doesn't mean it was Sean." She gave Callie a pleading look.

Callie sighed. "Sure, we all struggle with lots of people at innocent events we attend, right? Could have been anybody, really."

Iphy looked over the cake, a finger trailing over Sleeping Beauty's flowing hair. Then she sank down on a chair and burst out, "Truth is, it looks bad for him, Callie. Also, because he doesn't want to tell them what happened between him and the victim. I know him: once he's dead set on something, he won't change his mind again. He'll just sit there and say nothing and get Falk even madder at him."

"Falk isn't *mad* at him. He's doing his job." Callie noticed she was calling him Falk again, like she had in the beginning, as if they were strangers again and not . . . Maybe it would have been better if they had never gotten so close. If she had never expected he could care for her and feel how much she cared for him. It hurt to think about it, so Callie added hurriedly, "I'm sure Falk is very professional about handling this case, and especially Sean's part in it. He just can't help if a suspect won't cooperate. And you just mentioned how dead set Sean Strong can be, which isn't making it any easier." She waited a moment. "And are you sure he couldn't have been dead set on killing someone? If he felt he had a compelling reason?"

Iphy shook her head. "Sean may have strong opinions about things, but he loves his freedom. Can you see him behind bars?"

Callie considered this a moment. "Maybe he didn't think about that when he grabbed those scissors and stabbed the man he was arguing with. In a rage, you don't consider consequences—you just act."

"You think he's guilty?"

"I don't know. And I think you can't know either. You're basing your assessment of his character on your interactions with him . . . how many years ago?"

"Almost fifty," Iphy admitted. "People do change, I suppose . . ." Her voice trailed off, and a faraway look came to her eyes, as if she was suddenly remembering something.

"What?" Callie asked.

"Nothing. I'm sorry I got so emotional." Iphy forced a shaky laugh. She got to her feet, picked up the cake, and put it in the fridge. She waited a moment and then confided, "I do feel better now that you know, Callie. I just—I wasn't myself this morning when we left the police station, and I realized what desperate trouble Sean was in. I shouldn't have said that you're Falk's mouthpiece. I was so happy when you two got together, and I do wish you every happiness."

Callie's chest tightened at the idea that all happiness seemed further out of reach than ever. Ace was mad at her for various reasons, and although she knew matters were more nuanced than he had presented them to her, she did understand how he felt. How was she ever going to untangle it all again?

Did she even want to? Hadn't she been hurt deeply by his accusations, the sudden anger flaring at her? How much did Ace really care for her if he could say such hurtful things? If he didn't even find out whether he was in the right, but just said something?

Maybe she should just lean back and wait to see if he came to her and wanted to talk. If he offered the opening, he might be willing to really listen to her instead of jumping to conclusions because of something Peggy said or he thought Quinn had done. He didn't know half the facts!

Maybe she should just bide her time and see if it got better?

Chapter Fourteen

After Callie had locked Book Tea's door for the day and was putting a few chairs in place around the tables, there was a knock at that door, on the glass pane, an urgent knuckle rap. Callie spied Mrs. Forrester gesturing at her to let her in. She was looking about her as if she was being followed by someone she desperately wanted to escape.

Callie quickly unlocked the door, opened it, and let the library volunteer slip inside. While she was closing the door, Mrs. Forrester retreated to the back of Book Tea, pulling her coat tighter around her. She wasn't wearing the felt hat of the other day, with the diamond hatpin, but a close-fitting red model that vied with her flushed face for deepest color.

Callie asked her in a whisper what was wrong. Mrs. Forrester tried to catch her breath. "I knew you'd close up around this time. I hurried over here from the library."

"I thought the library closed an hour before we do," Callie said, puzzled. Mrs. Forrester nodded. "We do, but I often stay behind to tidy a bit. Tonight I also wanted to use the computer to look into something. My old one at home isn't that fast." She looked about her as if she feared that even here, inside Book Tea, unwelcome ears would be listening in on her revelations.

"What did you want to look into?" Callie asked. The woman's secretive behavior piqued her curiosity. This had to be about more than just wanting to fact-check something. Mrs. Forrester gestured for her to come over, and when they stood side by side, she said, "Remember how at the event several local people came to have their books appraised?"

"Yes, that was what it was for, right?" Callie didn't really understand what Mrs. Forrester was driving at.

"Well, I couldn't help myself—books are my forte, you know—so I kept an eye on what they were handing in and what they got for it. I noticed that our expert"—she spoke the word with a certain disdain—"wasn't exactly offering much. Of course people may believe their garage sale find is worth a fortune when in reality it's a quite common book or has some damage devaluing it."

"Yes, yes," Callie said, eager to get on with the story.

"This afternoon in the library, I heard that one couple is trying to get their book back."

"That's right. I saw someone at the police station asking for her book. It came from her mother's inheritance, I think."

"Exactly. Now I asked her to describe the book to me in detail, and she did. Then, after closing hours, I put all that information into the computer to see what I could find. It wasn't easy, as you have to know exactly what sites to look at and how to combine information."

Callie held the woman's gaze. "And?"

"Guess." Mrs. Forrester crossed her arms over her chest with a triumphant expression on her face. Now that she was standing still, the high color in her cheeks had died down a bit, but she was obviously still very excited.

Callie frowned. "I know the expert gave them twenty bucks. Should it have been fifty?" Mrs. Forrester scoffed.

"Eighty then?" Callie conjectured, thinking it would be rather rude of their expert to offer people less than one-fourth of what a book was really worth. But maybe he figured he would have to go to some trouble to sell it again and had to be recompensed for his time and effort?

"More like one hundred and fifty," Mrs. Forrester said. "Maybe more. That depends on the book's exact condition. I can't assess that without having held it in my hands, of course."

She leaned over. "But do you understand what this means? Our expert was cheating people!"

Callie pulled a doubtful expression. "I'm not sure you can call it cheating."

Mrs. Forrester harrumphed. "After I checked this one book and found this discrepancy, I started calling other people whom I had seen there, and asked them about the books they had handed in to Mr. King and what they had gotten for them. I then tried to find more information about the possible value of their books online. In several cases, the price mentioned on antique book sites or for auctions is considerably higher than what this man offered. I do admit that prices can vary, and it also depends on the interest in a particular piece, but still . . . What if Mr. King was abusing our event to get his hands on precious volumes for cheap?"

Callie still wasn't convinced. "But he was a well-known expert on old books. He even made his TV debut recently. Why would he risk ruining his reputation by doing something so unethical?"

"Because he obviously believed he could get away with it. He would only be here for an afternoon, then leave again. Even if people believed they might have been underpaid, where would they complain? You don't go to the police for something like that. You'd only feel silly. And they wouldn't do anything about it either."

Callie exhaled in a huff. Mrs. Forrester was probably right about that. If you figured you had been cheated, you would keep it to yourself, not wanting to look foolish in the community. Several people might have been cheated but probably wouldn't discuss this with one another so that the extent of it would stay under wraps. She thought for a moment. "Have you contacted the police about this?"

"I'm not contacting them about anything soon," Mrs. Forrester said. "I'm happy they're engaged with another suspect."

She looked around her again and then continued. "It's a shame for this Mr. Strong really. Such an interesting gentleman. A good singer too."

Callie didn't want to discuss Sean Strong and returned to the matter of the books at once. "If you think the dead expert was somehow dishonest in his appraisals at our event, you have to tell the police. It could provide a motive for murder."

"I don't think someone came back to stab him in the chest over a book." Mrs. Forrester readjusted the big brooch pinned on her coat's lapel. "But now you know, you can do with it whatever you want. You know the police better than most of us do."

Callie flushed at this subtle stab. Mrs. Forrester said, "You can tell Deputy Falk if you think he needs to know. But I doubt he'll do much about it. Mrs. Harris told me that when she went to the station to ask for her book back, she was almost turned out like a dog. Shameful."

"She didn't explain that her book had been deliberately undervalued and that it might have been Mr. King's common practice," Callie said in defense of the deputy who had handled the query. He had merely concluded that the old lady was sorry for a hasty sale, and he had been right mentioning to Callie that there was very little to be done about it.

Mrs. Forrester snorted. "She needn't have told them everything—that was for them to find out! What are the police for? To look into things and ensure the truth is discovered. But they're arresting people on a whim and then sitting there writing up reports or something." She looked Callie over. "You should know. At least they talk to you."

Callie felt like her face was on fire now. "Thank you for dropping by to tell me this. Have you got any proof of it? I mean—"

"Of course." Mrs. Forrester nodded and clicked open her purse. She extracted some sheets of letter-size paper that were folded into halves. "I printed off the most essential information. It gives the websites it comes from in a neat printed line on the bottom. So convenient. Then they can look for more if they want to." It sounded like she doubted they would want to.

Callie hesitated to accept the folded sheets. "If you have this printed off and it's clear-cut material, you could simply put it in the police station's letter box. Or scan the documents and email them."

"You do it." Mrs. Forrester shoved the papers into her hand. "They listen to you. It's sad that citizens get so little credit from official channels, but as long as they listen to someone, I suppose . . ." She looked Callie up and down as if to assess her and then said, "You've solved murders before. This is in good hands with you."

Maybe Callie should feel flattered, but she only had a sensation of panic that she was getting deeper and deeper into the case Falk had told her to leave alone. They had fought over it, even . . . broken up over it?

Had their relationship ended?

She wasn't even sure!

Mrs. Forrester marched to the door. "High time I get home and fix myself some dinner. I've been up and about all day long. You have a closer look at that, and see what you can do with it. Perhaps the police can get it as a last resort? If your own inquiries don't work out?" She winked at her, unbolted the door, and left.

Callie stood there, perplexed and annoyed that she had let the persuasive woman talk her into this. But she couldn't deny a certain interest in what the dead expert had been up to and how big his scheme had actually been. It did seem odd that Mrs. Forrester had unearthed such discrepancies between money offered and what those books were really worth.

She went to check on the door and bolt it again, and then sat down at a table to smooth the sheets and study their contents. Mrs. Forrester had printed off the estimated value from several sites where books and other antiques were appraised and auctioned off. She had also written down the information provided by the sellers. Comparing the two, it was easy to see that the prices asked for online were always far higher than what the expert had given the sellers.

But was this a common practice? Did it maybe feel like cheating but was in fact normal in the antiques business? People had to make a profit, right?

Callie leaned back and rubbed her forehead. Iphy had already said she wanted to talk to Seth Delacorte again, and holding this information, Callie felt a conversation with the assistant could indeed be very enlightening.

But if she went to the Cliff Hotel and spoke with him, she would be doing the exact thing Ace hated. Interfering, sticking her nose where it didn't belong.

She folded the sheets again, undecided. Normally, she would drive out to Ace's cabin and give him the sheets, pressing upon him how important it was to look into this. She would trust that he would do it because he was a conscientious man who loved his job.

But right now her relationship with Ace wasn't exactly friendly, and she wondered if he would simply ignore this information if she brought it to his attention. After all, he believed she had made Peggy unhappy and was somehow responsible for the whole thing with Quinn.

Callie grimaced. It wouldn't be easy to ever explain all of that. Especially after Ace had openly told Quinn he never wanted him around his sister and the boys, feelings were on edge. One more wrong move and . . .

She walked into the kitchen, where Iphy was putting the last load of dirty dishes and cups into the dishwasher. She looked up, and Callie saw her eyes were red-rimmed.

"What's wrong?" she asked at once, reaching out to put an arm around her great-aunt's narrow shoulders.

"I just heard from Sean's attorney," Iphy said in a shivering voice. "Because he's not cooperating, making a statement about the argument he had with the dead man, they're holding him. He is now officially being charged with the murder."

Iphy grabbed Callie's hand. "Do you understand what this means? They're no longer just suspecting him, interrogating him, with a chance he'll be released again once they discover it wasn't him. No—they have enough to charge him and hold him. That means they won't be looking for other suspects anymore. Falk believes he's closed the case."

Callie looked at her great-aunt's panicky expression. They had never had quite this situation before. People under suspicion, yes; taken to the station for questioning, yes; even held for a few hours, yes. But officially charged?

And Iphy was right that Ace would not be looking for other suspects if he believed he had his killer locked up.

Iphy said softly, "What's that?" She looked at the sheets Callie was holding.

Callie wanted to say "nothing special" and whisk them away, but her great-aunt's despair at her old flame's predicament forced her to speak up. "Mrs. Forrester just came by. She stayed at the library after closing to look into something she found suspicious." Callie quickly explained what the observant library volunteer had suspected and discovered, showing her the information on the sheets Mrs. Forrester had provided her with.

Iphy clapped her hands together. "But that's great! It proves the victim was a fraud. He might have been confronted by someone who was defrauded, and that person killed him. We must find out right away if Delacorte recognized people from earlier events being there as well. Someone who decided to—yes! Remember, Delacorte had that note, saying that if King came to Heart's Harbor it would bring him bad luck? It must all be related!"

Callie barely listened to the rest of what Iphy explained to her as she suddenly remembered the women in the parking lot. Saying something about just desserts.

Had they been involved somehow? But she had only seen them in passing and didn't know their names or where they had come from. It seemed like a loose end they couldn't pursue.

Iphy pinched her arm, bringing her back to the present. "Don't you think?"

"What?" Callie asked sheepishly.

Iphy shook her head. "Are you listening or not? We have to talk to Delacorte."

"Ace doesn't want me to get involved."

"And you just listen to Ace?" Iphy sounded indignant. "He has the wrong suspect in custody. He messed up, and he refuses to see it."

"You just told me that Strong won't make any statement. That does make him look pretty suspicious. Why won't he cooperate?"

Iphy's expression darkened. "I don't know. It worries me." She rubbed her arms as if she were cold. "I just have to do something. Anything."

Callie came to a decision. "All right. We'll go see Delacorte together. We don't know if he's involved somehow—I mean, in Mr. King's possibly dubious activities—so it's better if you don't go alone. You never know."

Iphy nodded and went to get her coat. Callie looked at Daisy, who was eyeing her expectantly, perhaps hoping to go out on a walk. "What do you think, girl? Am I doing the right thing?" She hoped Ace would never find out about this.

A stab inside her made her wince, but she couldn't go back on her given word now. She told Daisy to be a good girl while they were away, and they left.

* * *

At the Cliff Hotel, dinner was in full swing. Iphy asked for Mr. Delacorte and was directed to his table. He was sitting alone, dressed in a nice but quiet suit, just starting on his main course. He rose to his feet when he recognized them and pointed at the chairs opposite. "Do sit down. Would you care to join me? The hotel takes non-guest diners."

"Why not?" Iphy said, and the waiter who had hovered nearby closed in at once to take their orders. Callie chose broccoli soup as an opener and Iphy, carpaccio. Delacorte said, "I also had the carpaccio. It's excellent."

Last time, dressed in his pajamas, he had looked younger and unbalanced, but here, at dinner, he seemed more in control and even a bit wary of them. Callie wondered if Falk, upon taking Delacorte's statement, had impressed on him that he wasn't to discuss the case with inquisitive locals. She felt her cheeks flame at the idea.

Iphy said, "I hope you feel a bit better after the dreadful events."

Delacorte nodded. "I'm glad the killer has been apprehended. I felt unsafe with him being on the loose."

"Suspected killer," Callie corrected. "We don't know yet if he really did it."

"He must have. He fought with my boss. The medical examiner even found marks of it on the body."

"How do you know that?" Iphy asked, her eyes wide, as if she was impressed.

"I talked to someone at the police station. I was afraid of being targeted as well. But they assured me that the attack was aimed at my boss solely and not at me." He pricked his fork into a small round potato covered in herbs.

Iphy said, "Why were you afraid to be targeted as well?"

Delacorte shrugged. "Sometimes people aren't happy with the way in which goods are appraised. They come back later and make threats. But I never expected it to get this violent."

"You did know he was being threatened," Callie said. "You kept that note saying Heart's Harbor would bring him bad luck."

He nodded slowly. "I keep all of those notes. I just felt like I should. Like putting them in the trash would be something criminal almost. I'm responsible for the paperwork and—"

"Did you ever notice anything unusual?" Callie pounced. "Like maybe prices being too low?"

Delacorte studied her with a frown. "What do you mean 'too low'?"

"That what he offered people for books was below the real value."

"That is common practice. He has to sell them again and make a profit."

"By how much?"

"Excuse me?"

"By how much? What is the margin? Can I say buy a book for ten dollars and sell it again for twenty?"

Delacorte laughed softly. "That would be a 100% margin. You overestimate our work. We usually make ten percent. Sometimes a bit more if we have a good piece or someone entrusts us with an entire estate."

"People do that?" Iphy asked, glancing at Callie. Callie bet her great-aunt was thinking the same thing as she was: that left alone with an entire estate, a dishonest expert would have the ideal opportunity to make a bundle. Had King profited off dead people, and had the relatives found out later on?

"Oh yes, all the time." Delacorte seemed to start when the shadow of a passing waiter fell on the table. He reached up and straightened his tie. "If someone dies, and the relatives don't want to clean out the house, they can leave the whole thing to us. My boss used to put a price on the sum total, and then we'd clean out and sell everything, you know. People are so busy these days that they don't want to comb through old vases and broken lamps for weeks on end. You'd be amazed what elderly people collect. Most of it, worthless."

Most of it, but not all of it, Callie thought. She said, "Did you ever hit on something extra special among such an inheritance?"

Delacorte took his time answering, focusing on the steak he was cutting up. Then he said with a forced laugh, "If you mean if we ever uncovered something worth a fortune, not exactly, no. Most of the time it's just a lot of junk."

Callie glanced at Iphy to see if she also had the impression he wasn't being totally honest with them. But the waiter arrived with their order, and they thanked him. Callie took up her spoon and dipped it into the hot soup, breathing its spicy scent.

Iphy said, "But it must have been exciting every single time to go into such a house and look through the things. Like a treasure hunt. You can never know what you might find."

Delacorte smiled at her, an almost indulgent smile. "It seems more exciting than it is. You know, people are spoiled with these TV shows where locals come in, and they bring a plate or a sugar pot, and it turns out to be worth a lot. But do you have any idea how many people flock to such a day of appraisals and have absolutely nothing to show when they leave again? I think if you claimed that one person out of a hundred owns something of value, that would be a very positive estimate. And when I say 'of value,' I'm not even talking about a five-figure sum. More likely a hundred bucks for a vase, you know. It's nice and all, but not life changing."

Callie hemmed. "So you don't think anything valuable was brought in at the Valentine's event here in Heart's Harbor?"

Delacorte shrugged. "I wouldn't know, really. I'm just the assistant. I do the paperwork."

"For how long now?"

"Four years."

"In that time, you must have picked up some things, gotten a bit of expert knowledge of your own."

Delacorte shook his head. "My boss didn't treat me like an apprentice who was learning a trade. He never explained his decisions or his appraisals. They were as mystifying to me as to anyone."

"And you didn't feel the urge to learn more yourself?" Callie asked, perplexed. Having traveled the world for years, she had always longed to learn more about each place she went, pick up tidbits of local history, and expand her knowledge. She couldn't imagine working for someone and simply accepting his decisions about antique goods without ever trying to learn more oneself.

Delacorte said, "I have to be honest with you. Antiques aren't really my thing. I was in college as a law student when my father lost his job and could no longer pay for my tuition. I had to find a job on short notice to make ends meet, and then I came across Mr. King's advertisement. I applied and he took me on. First, for a trial period, where he wanted to see if I worked neatly enough for him. I was good with figures, so he kept me on. That's the whole story. It's not hard work, and it pays decent wages, plus the traveling is nice. I get to see quite a bit of the country."

Callie nodded, and Iphy said, "I'm sorry to hear about your father's job. I do hope he's found something again?"

Delacorte looked at his plate. "He died."

"Oh, I'm sorry I asked. My condolences."

Delacorte nodded curtly and then said, "You couldn't know." He looked up again with a sad smile. "My father was part of the reason I went to law school in the first place. He so wanted me to be a lawyer. I didn't much care for it myself, but I wanted to please him."

Callie felt sorry for the young man's position, first having chosen a career for his father's sake and then, after his father's dismissal and a lack of money to complete his college education, having to look for some impromptu job. "So now that Mr. King is no longer here, what will you do?"

Delacorte sighed. "I'm not sure yet." He played with his fork.

Iphy glanced at Callie. Callie sensed her uneasiness and realized that it would be difficult to broach the topic they had come to discuss. Delacorte didn't seem to have the knowledge required to judge whether his boss had been dishonest in his appraisals, and as his boss had apparently not shared anything about the business side either, how would he know what had gone down?

"Oh," Delacorte said, "there they are." He nodded in the direction of the dining room's entrance.

Callie turned her head. Two ladies in nice dresses had entered and stood waiting for the waiter to direct them to a free table. One of them seemed vaguely familiar. That hair, the profile.

Suddenly, with a shock, Callie realized these two ladies were the ones she had seen in the parking lot discussing a man who would get his just desserts. The ones who had also been up in the book room to have something appraised.

"You know them?" she asked Delacorte.

"Not really, but they were at the event, to have my boss appraise some books for them. They acted very . . . uh . . ." Delacorte flushed. "Like they were interested in him."

"In a personal way?"

Delacorte nodded. "When I put away the book he bought from one of them, a card fell out. It said 'Paula,' with a hotel room number and the words 'Tonight at ten.'"

"A rendezvous?" Callie asked, glancing at the ladies, who were now taking their seats. They didn't look like the casual dating types. But then again, how could you tell?

Delacorte said, "My boss could turn on the charm if he wanted to. I guess he already knew them from a prior occasion. He did seem a bit flustered when they were at his table."

"How odd," Iphy said. She obviously had trouble not staring at the ladies.

"And which one of them is Paula?" Callie asked.

"The one on the left. The younger one with the blonde hair." Delacorte frowned hard, as if trying to recall something. "Her hotel room number was 408."

Iphy exchanged a quick look with Callie. Callie bet she knew what her great-aunt was thinking. That as soon as they were done dining with Delacorte, they had to find out more about the mysterious Paula and her friend.

Chapter Fifteen

It was a great thing they had decided to dine with Delacorte, because it had offered them the perfect excuse to be at the hotel. After their soup and carpaccio, Callie had salmon with mixed vegetables, and Iphy chose a quiche with four kinds of cheese. Delacorte told them several funny stories of his appraisal days, and at one point as Callie sipped her mineral water, she thought that without the murder this could have been a very pleasant evening.

For dessert, Iphy had coffee with bonbons while Callie chose ice cream with meringue. She kept a careful eye on Paula and her companion, who, despite having started eating later, had caught up with them and were also eating dessert. Chocolate mousse, it seemed, from the tall glasses. While they were eating, they seemed to have fallen into a discussion of some kind, Paula turning paler and quieter while her companion talked more and gestured about her.

Just as their glasses were almost empty, the companion, red in the face and jerky in her movements, got up, shoving her chair so far back it almost knocked into a passing waiter, and said something, then left with her head held high. Paula stayed seated, looking at her disappearing friend with a shocked expression. She seemed to want to take the last bites of her mousse, then seemed to decide against it, put the spoon back in the glass, collected her bag, and left as well.

"Mr. Delacorte," Iphy said, "you've been a charming host for the night. Thanks so much, but we must be leaving now. Goodbye."

And she rose and walked off.

Callie got to her feet as well, grabbed for her handbag, which dangled off her chair, and said goodbye to Delacorte. He didn't seem stunned by their abrupt departure, and something of a smile tugged at the corners of his mouth as if he knew they were going after Paula and her nameless friend.

Callie felt a bit embarrassed that their actions were so transparent. She told a passing waiter that she'd like to pay the bill, pulling out her wallet and not twitching a muscle when the steep price was quoted. The Cliff Hotel was a fancy place to dine, and you had to expect a matching price tag.

Still, it took her a few minutes to get it all settled, and when she walked out into the lobby, Iphy was nowhere to be seen.

Looking about her, slightly lost, Callie recalled that Delacorte had given Paula's room number as 408, and made her way up to the fourth floor. There she found Iphy in the corridor, looking at a door.

Spotting Callie, Iphy at once gestured for her to come over, and said in a whisper, "I wanted to make sure she didn't elude us. She went inside."

She looked Callie over. "What should we do? Just knock and ask if we can talk to her?"

"For what reason? Because she came to offer a book for appraisal at our Valentine's event?" Callie shifted her weight. "She put a card in the book, inviting Mr. King for a meeting here. Something quite . . . uh . . . intimate. Maybe she's a former girlfriend? She won't tell us a thing."

Iphy sighed. "Maybe not. But this is a lead. An ignored lead, I might add. Falk hasn't done a thorough job."

"Well, if Delacorte didn't tell him about Paula, how was he to know?" Callie felt obliged to defend Ace, also a bit out of guilt as she realized she hadn't told him about the women in the parking lot discussing someone's just desserts. It had seemed a bit vague and irrelevant, but combined with Delacorte's statements now . . .

Iphy seemed to have come to a decision because she nodded to herself and approached the door. She knocked. The sound reverberated across Callie's tight nerve endings.

It took a moment, then a female voice asked from inside, "Sylvia, is that you?"

Iphy glanced at Callie and replied, "Yes."

Callie cringed under this outright lie to gain access to the woman, but it was too late already. The door opened, and the room's occupant appeared on the threshold. Her eyes widened when she saw them.

Iphy smiled. "Good evening. I would really—"

When the woman tried to shut the door, Iphy quickly moved into the doorway. "I would really like to talk to you."

"I asked if you were Sylvia," the woman spat. "You said yes."

"I didn't hear you properly," Iphy lied cheerfully. "It's about the book you offered to the expert at Haywood Hall. It was worth more than he offered to pay you. We're here to set the balance straight."

Callie wasn't sure that more lying would help their case, but Paula seemed relieved it was just about a book. She stood there undecided for a moment, then she stepped back. "Do come in. Don't look at the mess."

What mess she meant eluded Callie, as the room was perfectly neat. No suitcases in sight, no clothes lying around. Nothing on the nightstand.

Iphy said, "I'm sorry this is a bit awkward, coming to your hotel room so late. But we spent quite some time tracking everybody."

Paula laughed, a short nervous laugh. "I'm surprised you could track me at all."

Callie held her gaze. "That wasn't so hard. You left a card in the book, giving your name and hotel room number."

Paula flushed. "I did? Oh yes, now I remember. I thought that maybe if the book interested him, he would want more, and then he could contact me."

"You have more of such books?"

"Yes, from an aunt." Paula nodded. "She died, and I don't know what to do with it all, really." She gestured around her. "I'm a stewardess. I'm abroad a lot. I don't need a ton of things."

"I see." Callie pointed at some leather chairs by a fake fireplace. "May I sit down?"

"Certainly." Paula gestured to Iphy to take a seat as well. "How unhospitable of me when you went through such trouble to find me. The book is worth more, you say? What a surprise. I thought it was quite a nice offer already."

"How much did he pay you?"

"Forty. It was a large leather-bound volume, but very old, and there was some wear and tear."

"If it was very old," Callie asked, puzzled, "didn't you wonder if forty was the right price?"

"That's why I went to an expert, right?" Paula widened her eyes. "If I had just offered it online or something, I would have wondered if I had gotten the right price for it, but not now. He knew his stuff." She opened the drawer of the night-stand and then froze. "Oh, I keep forgetting I'm not at home." She closed the drawer again.

"But you travel widely, right?" Callie asked. She had an unsettling feeling the woman wasn't being completely honest.

Paula said, "What went wrong with the book sale? Am I entitled to more money? I really don't need it, you know. I have enough from my job."

"Still, you came all the way out here to sell a book for forty dollars," Iphy said quietly.

Paula fidgeted with her hands. "Just because it seemed so rude not to do anything with the inheritance. I never knew my aunt well, but she left everything to me, so she deserved some consideration."

"I see. You wanted the expert to also buy the other things included in this inheritance?"

"Well, it would have made it easier for me to settle it. Not being around much and all." Paula paced the room. "You see, now that Mr. King is . . . uh . . . no longer here, I guess he can't help me, and I'll just have to go back home. You can keep the money you think he should have given me for the book. It's really not that—"

A loud knock at the door made her jerk. She stood frozen, glancing from Iphy and Callie to the door and back.

The knocking came again, more urgently. She went over and hissed, "Not now."

"I have to talk to you," a female voice said. "I'm sorry about what I just said. We have to pull this off."

Paula stood with her hand pressed against the door like she wanted to push right through the wood and shove the other woman away. "I can't talk to you now."

"Nonsense. Open up."

Paula swallowed audibly and opened the door. The woman who had been with her in the dining room marched in. Then she saw Iphy and Callie. "Who are they?"

"They're here to give me some extra money for the book I brought in. It seems it wasn't appraised properly."

A flash of something crossed the woman's face, as if she wasn't surprised at all at the idea of fraud at the event. "Well, well," she said, studying Iphy and Callie. "Got afraid now that he's dead? Quickly return the money to the duped parties before the police hear about it?"

"Sylvia!" Paula whispered, but Sylvia pushed on. "It's despicable how you betray innocent people with events like this. Come and have your books appraised. Come and be ripped off, you mean."

"You knew the expert betrayed people?" Callie asked.

Sylvia scoffed at her. "Don't act innocent with me. I know exactly what King was like. How he treated people. And how he charmed women. Which one of you was he dating? Or both? It didn't matter to him."

"Sylvia," Paula said again. "Just let them give me back the money they think they owe me and be done with it."

Iphy shook her head. "If you know more about this fraudulent activity, you should talk to the police."

"The police?" Sylvia's voice rose. "I talked to the police all right, and they just laughed at me. They thought I had been a silly goose. They couldn't do anything for me, they said. That taught me about the police." She stood up straight, her hands by her side clenching and unclenching.

A strong woman, Callie thought, *and someone who would carry a grudge.*

Iphy said, "But this time it wasn't just fraud. It was murder as well."

"I'm not sorry he died," Sylvia said. "And I won't lift a finger to assist the police in solving it. Why? For justice for *him*?" She sounded as if she would like to spit on the floor to underline her words.

Iphy said, "Not for him, but for the man who has been arrested for the murder. He's innocent, and I intend to prove it and get him out."

Paula raised both hands to her face. "You're not here about the book." She glanced at Sylvia. "I told you not to—"

Sylvia ignored her. "We can't tell you anything about the murder. We just handed in the book, and then we went to the concert. We were nowhere near King when he died."

"But you came to Heart's Harbor on purpose to confront him?" Callie asked.

Paula said, "I came to have him appraise my book and maybe get my aunt's inheritance sorted." Her voice was thin with a hint of desperate insistence.

Callie said, "The police can check whether you really have an aunt who died recently. They can also check whether you're actually a stewardess like you claim. If you've been lying, that won't look good."

Paula cast Sylvia a pleading look.

Sylvia sighed. Then she said, "I told you that stupid lie about your aunt's inheritance wouldn't go far."

"We could have pulled it off if he hadn't been killed." Paula stamped her foot. "Imagine him having to die just when we're around."

Sylvia grimaced. "It's like he's conning us all over, this time from beyond the grave."

Callie said, "Can anyone please explain to me what this is about? You're obviously not just a woman looking for an expert to take her aunt's inheritance off her hands. But why did you come to see Mr. King?"

Paula looked at Sylvia. "Are we going to tell them?"

Sylvia shook her head. "Why would we? They have nothing against us."

Iphy said, "Callie here is the fiancé of the local deputy who is currently replacing the sheriff, who is in bed with a concussion. If she tells him what she learned here, Falk will be at the hotel in a flash to take you in for questioning. Your lies will get out soon enough, and then . . ." She clucked her tongue.

Sylvia eyed Callie in disbelief. "The fiancé of the local law officer?"

Iphy pulled out her cell phone. "I can call him now if you want to verify it."

Callie held her breath, imagining a call coming in asking Ace to confirm that she was his fiancé, when they had just about broken up. What would he say?

Sylvia released her breath. "Don't call. We believe you." She glanced at Paula. "And we will tell you what happened. If you keep us out of the murder investigation. We had nothing to do with it. On my honor."

Iphy put her phone back into her pocket. "Out with it then."

Paula looked at Sylvia. "Should I . . .?"

Before she could finish her sentence, Sylvia shook her head abruptly and began talking. "Eight years ago I met a charming man. He was kind, understanding, he took me out. He paid the bills, held open the door—a true gentleman. He told me great stories about his travels, his yacht in the Mediterranean. I adored him. Then one night he came to me in a panic. His credit card had been stolen, and someone had been using it. He needed to fly out to the other side of the country to set it straight, in person, but he had no access to money. He wondered if I could lend him some. For the airplane ticket, a hotel, taxis, and more. I was so sorry for him, I loaned him two thousand dollars. In cash."

Sylvia laughed softly. "After a day or two, he called me. He couldn't get it resolved quickly, and he needed more money. I wired him another two thousand dollars. You can imagine how this played out. More stories, more drama, and more money. When he had ten thousand dollars of my money, he never called me again."

Callie sat motionless, picturing how hurt and embarrassed Sylvia must have felt.

"I went to the police. Once there and being questioned, I realized how little I actually knew about him. He had given me a fake name of course, and I had never been to his house. I didn't know where he worked exactly—something in stocks he told me, but I didn't need to worry my pretty head over the details. You get the idea." Sylvia laughed bitterly. "They said they couldn't do much with this information, and I had given him the money of my own accord. No coercion, no blackmail or anything."

She stared at the floor. "I told myself when I left the police station that I would remember his face. And if I ever came across him again, I would go after him to get my money back."

Sylvia took a deep breath. "Now I'm not the only one who had this experience. You can regularly read such stories in magazines or newspapers. So one day I was reading a magazine where several duped women told their story, and one of those stories matched mine right down to the details. Including the nicknames the man had given during the fake relationship."

Sylvia clenched her hands. "I felt humiliated all over again but also determined to get this pig. Via the magazine,

I got in touch with this other woman. We compared notes, but since he used fake names, we couldn't track him. We hired a PI, and we also put out calls online to find more women who had been duped."

Sylvia paced the room again. "In the end, we found out he was now an expert in old books, and decided to come here to confront him. Paula would, with her story of the inheritance, tempt him to come to her hotel room at night. Then I would be here as well, to give him a piece of my mind."

"And to get your money back," Callie added.

Sylvia nodded. "We were going to give him a choice: pay us back or face charges."

"But he would have known, just like you knew, that you could never prove it was him." Callie held Sylvia's gaze.

"We counted on him wanting to avoid charges at all costs. He has a reputation to protect now that he's been on TV." Sylvia sounded disparaging. "It would have worked. Had he been able to come."

"But he was already dead," Iphy said. "And why invite him to your hotel room? You could have confronted him at the event."

"Why? It would have worked much better here." Sylvia gestured around her. "Not somewhere where other people might intervene. He had this assistant who followed him like a puppy."

Callie said, "You just said you were going to let Paula go to the event and invite King here. But you went with her. You were with her when she offered her book for appraisal.

I saw both of you in the bookroom, and he didn't recognize you then?"

She noticed Paula made a nervous movement. Sylvia said, "Of course not, it was years ago. And we took care to look different. He wasn't supposed to know what was up until he was in here."

Iphy asked, "And after you had given him the book with the invitation in it, you didn't see him again? Neither of you went back up to confront him, one on one?"

Sylvia shook her head. "Why would we have done that? Everything had gone so well, it was just a matter of time. Wait patiently until he showed up here and paid his dues."

His just desserts, Callie thought.

"But he never came," Sylvia said, "so nothing happened here. We don't know who killed him."

Paula seemed to want to say something but changed her mind. She stood with her head down.

Sylvia continued, "Now I have told you all I know. Please leave."

"You should tell your story to the police," Iphy urged. "Once they know he was a conman before, they can widen their circle of inquiries."

"Yes—to us, you mean." Sylvia laughed softly. "I don't think so. You have nothing concrete against us."

She glanced at Callie. "Your fiancé can't do anything with vague leads. And he might just lose his job if he goes after people because someone who isn't with the police blabbered. You know, I wonder if it's even legal for a deputy to send his fiancée to someone in the privacy of their hotel room and put pressure on them to confess to some imagined crime."

Callie, who sensed where this was going, rose to her feet. "We're leaving. Thanks for your time."

Iphy seemed to want to protest, but Callie gestured at her to come along to the door.

Sylvia accompanied them and said, "I'm sorry King caused trouble at your event. But that was just the man he was. Trouble wherever he went. Good night."

As soon as Callie and Iphy stepped outside, she closed the door behind them. They heard it lock.

Iphy said, "I wasn't done yet. We could have convinced them to—"

"Of course not. They had a bad experience with the police when they tried to report how they were duped. They don't believe in justice."

"Either of them might have killed the victim. I bet it was one of them and not Sean." Iphy pouted. "But how are we going to prove it?"

Callie sighed. There was only one way, and she saw it clearly. The only problem was, she didn't want to go down that route right now. The route to the police station.

After all, Paula had left a card in the book she had sold to the dead expert. As the belongings of the dead man had been put in the police's keeping, Ace could claim he had found the card in there and followed up on it. Paula could never prove otherwise. And once this factual lead had put Paula and Sylvia on Ace's radar, he could look closer at them and their movements at the event.

But Callie knew she had little to no leeway with Ace at the moment, and besides, Sylvia's threats to endanger Ace's career had hit her hard. If he lost what he had built because of her, he'd certainly never forgive her. They'd never be together again, sit like they had over breakfast, feeling at peace together.

She blinked hard against the burn behind her eyes. It was all steering toward disaster, and she had no idea how to get things back on course toward a solution.

Iphy looked her over. "What are you thinking? That Sean won't be cleared?" She sounded so dejected it hurt Callie's heart. She took in her great-aunt's appearance, her fragile figure that had seemed to grow more vulnerable over the past few days. Once upon a time, Iphy had decided against a chance for happiness because of loyalty to her family—a concept Callie understood all too well. What was a little hurt, confronting Ace, if she could try and help this beloved woman save the man she had once cared for? Didn't Iphy deserve her unquestioning support?

Callie straightened up and checked her watch. Normally, Ace would be home by now, but she knew that when he was frustrated, he liked to stay at the station and work until late into the night. She bet they could still find him there.

And either way, she wasn't going to take her great-aunt to his cabin. There were too many memories attached to happier moments spent there. "We're going to the police station. I've got the perfect plan for how Ace can get to these wily ladies."

Chapter Sixteen

At the station they found a deputy preparing to leave, apparently in response to a call about a car theft in the parking lot of a highway restaurant. Ace was just giving him a few last instructions, telling him to call in for backup if he needed any. The deputy nodded and left, brushing past them, his car key in his hand. Ace saw them and froze.

Callie stood there just looking at his face, the lines around his mouth, the tiredness in his eyes, everything she knew so well and loved about him. She felt terrible for what had happened to them, and still she didn't know how to solve it, as it seemed to have happened, and—

"I don't have a lot of time," Ace said. His voice sounded chill and dismissive.

"Is Sean still here?" Iphy asked. "Or has he been transferred to . . .?" She swallowed.

"He's still here. His lawyer claims he can deliver proof of his innocence before eleven tomorrow morning. I thought it would be rather harsh to send an old man to jail." Ace leaned back, a silent challenge in his posture.

Iphy sighed with relief. "Oh, good, then we can talk right away."

A frown formed over Ace's eyes. "I just said I don't have a lot of time. His lawyer is working to get him cleared. Now you let it be."

He wanted to turn away from them, but Iphy said, "I doubt that the lawyer knows what we know. Please hear us out."

Ace looked her over, then glanced at Callie. "What have you got to say for yourself?"

Callie shrugged. "I know I can't ask for anything. But we do know a few things that you might not, and they could be important. Like you just said, Sean Strong is an old man, and he doesn't deserve to go to jail if he's innocent."

Ace stood and stared at the floor. The silence seemed to stretch forever.

Callie bit her lip and resisted the urge to fidget with her hands or shift her weight. She hadn't expected him to come up and hug her, but this coldness was terrible.

Then Ace said, "All right. I want to give everyone a fair chance." He gestured to the sheriff's office. "In there then."

Iphy went ahead, and Ace came to walk beside Callie. "I'm disappointed, though," he said in a low voice, "that you just continued sleuthing. You don't care about my opinion at all, do you?"

Callie wanted to protest, but they were already at the office door, and Ace made an exaggerated gesture for her to go in first.

Iphy had already taken a chair and began to rattle about Mrs. Forrester, the deception with the valuable books, and how her information had then put them on the trail of the women at the hotel.

Ace had taken a seat opposite, in the sheriff's heavy leather swivel chair, and listened with his hands folded on the edge of the desk. Callie saw that the information did strike him as peculiar and potentially relevant, and he was processing the possible leads and actions as he listened.

Finally Iphy said, "So you see there were people at the event who had every reason to hate our victim and come after him."

Ace said, "Yes, but the ladies assured you they wanted to confront the man away from other people, at the hotel. Why leave a card in a book, giving your name and room number, and then go and murder the man in question in a house crowded with people? That wouldn't be very smart."

"Well, apparently they *have* been very smart about their actions, because you don't have them locked up right now—you have Sean." Iphy sounded indignant.

Ace winced. "I haven't had time yet to comb through all of those books and other belongings. By the way, how did you know about the card and what it said?"

Callie winced as this was the painful point she had hoped Ace wouldn't ask about.

Iphy said, "From Seth Delacorte."

Ace threw his weight back in the chair, which creaked in protest. "You went to see him again? After I explained how I felt about that?" His eyes shot sparks at them, especially at Callie. "It was the only way. Iphy so wanted to clear Sean Strong." Callie pleaded with her eyes for him to understand how she had just wanted to help her great-aunt, someone she loved and would do anything for.

Ace sighed. "I can of course act like I found the card in the book when we checked it for evidence, and am following up on this lady called Paula to see what she can tell me about Mr. King."

"Yes, but you must talk to her while this Sylvia isn't present," Iphy said. "She takes the lead, does all the talking, and she seems rather shrewd. I think you can get more from Paula alone."

After a short silence she added, almost as an afterthought, "Besides, Sylvia was the one who threatened to ruin your career."

"What?" Ace asked.

Iphy feigned an innocent expression. "She thought she could threaten us into keeping our mouths shut by saying she would complain about you sending civilians to the hotel to ask questions. But we weren't there on your orders, so there's no problem really, is there?"

"And why would she even *think* I had sent you there?" Ace asked, his brows knitting.

Iphy fidgeted with her bracelet. "Because I may have let it slip that Callie was . . . seeing you. To put a bit of pressure on them."

Ace tilted his head. "You didn't," he said.

"I did." Iphy sounded small. "It was just because this Sylvia was so smug, acting like nothing could touch her. I guess, in the heat of the moment, things like that slip out. And it's not a lie."

Ace shot Callie a look. She hoped he wasn't going to reveal to her great-aunt here and now that it was over between them. "I'm sorry," Iphy said in a thin, brittle voice. "I just can't help thinking Sean will end up in jail and lose everything he has. His reputation, his freedom. I have no idea why he refuses to tell you anything, but there must be a reason for it. Something other than guilt. I can't work out what it is, but please have a closer look to see if you can find any way to clear him. Please."

In the bright light of the lamp overhead, she looked very pale and worn, and Callie hoped Ace would see this too and feel forgiving toward her.

Ace released his breath in a huff. Whether it was irritation or resignation was hard to say. "That woman you spoke to—Sylvia—threatened my career?"

"Sylvia acted like if you came after her she would file charges of some sort that you had acted unprofessionally, sending us over to . . . uh . . . put pressure on her. That was about the gist of what she said, right, Callie?" Nervously knotting her fingers, Iphy looked at Callie for support.

Callie said, "I guess she felt bad about having told us too much and wanted to ensure we kept it to ourselves."

"But you aren't keeping it to yourselves; you're here now, putting me on the spot." Ace jumped to his feet and paced the room. "If I do go after her and she makes trouble for me . . ."

Callie glanced at Iphy. There wasn't really anything they could say to that.

Iphy asked, “Is Sean all right? Can I see him for a moment? I only want to ask him why he’s not cooperating with you.”

Ace looked her over. Then he said, “I’ll bring him in here, and you can talk with him. In my presence. I’m not letting him slip by me.”

Iphy sat up and nodded eagerly. “I won’t do anything to help him flee, Deputy. Honestly.”

Ace looked at Callie as if to find some truth about this statement in her eyes. Then he left the room.

Her heart pounding, Callie slipped to the edge of her seat and said, “You aren’t going to help him escape, are you?” Normally, she wouldn’t have expected anything like that from her great-aunt, but Iphy wasn’t herself these days.

“Of course not. Then he would be on the run, wanted. That would only make it worse for him.”

Callie tilted her head and studied her great-aunt closely. She wasn’t entirely sure she could believe her. After all, Ace had agreed to keep Strong out of jail until the next morning, but after that, all bets were off. What if Iphy believed she had to somehow prevent Strong from ending up behind bars? It would be a disastrous action, which wouldn’t only hurt Strong’s case but also get Iphy in trouble with the law.

Footsteps approached and the door opened. Ace let in Sean Strong. He was dressed in a dark sweater and black pants, and looked like he had been awoken from a nap. He stood there quietly, watching Iphy. She got to her feet and seemed to want to rush over to him, but he made a gesture to stop her. "I'm not happy to see you. You shouldn't have come here to bother the deputy. Iphy, please, just leave this to my lawyer."

Iphy winced at the word *bother*. "I have information that can help you."

"I don't need your help." Strong looked at Ace. "Take me back to the cell."

"These ladies have gone through a lot of trouble for you," Ace said. "I think you can at least have the decency to speak with them for a few minutes."

Strong exhaled in a huff. "I don't have to speak with anyone. Not with you either." He glared at Iphy. "You have no idea what's at stake here."

"Don't I? You're accused of murder. You'll be transferred to prison soon. You'll be locked up with real criminals. Even though you are innocent. I will do anything to prove that. Even put myself in danger."

There was a flash in Strong's eyes. He glanced at Ace. "The deputy won't let you."

Ace laughed softly. "These ladies have solved two murders before, Mr. Strong. I wouldn't dismiss them too easily. And for your information, they don't listen to me. *At all.*"

The latter words were underlined with a sharp look at Callie, who lowered her eyes.

"Two murders?" Strong looked confused. "Who died, and when, and why were you involved?"

"That doesn't really matter now." Iphy came over and took his hand in hers. "I want to help you, Sean. I know you think you don't need help, but you do. For once shed that stubbornness of yours and—"

"We found out some important information," Callie added. "That the dead man swindled people. That could provide a motive for murder."

"Exactly," Strong said in an ominous tone. He pulled his hand away from Iphy and stood there, straight and almost glowering.

Suddenly Callie understood. It came to her in a painful flash as she realized with breathless intensity what this meant. How Iphy's attempts to help Sean Strong had achieved the exact opposite. "You were a victim too? You came to confront him about his actions? You exchanged places with Teak specifically to . . .?"

Iphy raised both hands to her face. "Oh, Sean." She looked at Callie, struggling to speak without shivering. "We unearthed his motive for murder!"

Strong laughed softly. "That was my reason for not wanting to speak with your deputy. But it's too late now."

Iphy looked devastated. "We only made it worse," she whispered to no one in particular. "This is the end of it."

Ace put a hand on Strong's shoulder. "Won't you take a seat, sir? Then we can talk." After a short silence, he continued, "You can now freely tell us your story."

Strong hesitated a moment and then walked to the chair Iphy had vacated. "Why not?" He sat down and sighed. "I guess it would have to come out sooner or later. I was just hoping I could keep her out of it." He sat there with his head down.

Iphy came to stand beside him and put her arm around him. He didn't stir.

Ace sat down in the sheriff's swivel chair again. He didn't press the man to speak, but waited quietly until he began talking of his own accord. "I'm in my seventies, Deputy. Most people that age no longer have their parents. But my mother had me at a very young age. She was a strong woman who fought through every setback life threw at her: the death of my father when she had five children to care for, a perpetual lack of money. She never complained but was always trying to see the bright side of things. All of us took odd jobs at a young age to help her make ends meet. Then, when we were older, she married again. A wealthy businessman who owned several factories in the region, and at last she had a good life. I left home and pursued my singing career, and I'm ashamed to admit I didn't see her often."

Callie recalled Iphy had told her that back then, when they had first met, when asked about his family, Sean had said that he wasn't in touch with them much.

Strong continued in a low voice, "But three years ago her second husband died as well, and she was left alone again. She was a woman with a good heart, but no head for money. She left the financial side of things to her bankers and accountants. And then Mr. King came into her life."

Throwing back his head to stare up at the ceiling, Strong clenched his hands together. "I was always traveling, and I didn't look after her like I should. I thought my sisters were visiting her, you know, and I had no idea how lonely she really was. How much she ached for someone to just be kind to her."

Callie swallowed, picturing this vulnerable elderly lady. Easy prey?

"I don't know how they met exactly, or how he managed to win her confidence. But she let him into her life, her home, and he defrauded her of several valuable art objects. It wasn't just the value of them but also the humiliation of having trusted someone and then being betrayed. Her heart couldn't take it. She died."

He looked up, his eyes burning with indignation. "I found out about the fraud because the lawyers had compared lists of what she owned with the actual objects in her home, and there was a discrepancy. I knew my mother would never sell things off without others knowing about it, so I asked her neighbors whether they had noticed anything in the months leading up to her death. That's how I found out about the handsome well-dressed man visiting her. One neighbor recalled a license plate, and with the help of a PI, I traced him. Our expert." He said it in a venomous tone.

Ace was listening quietly, not making notes, just sitting there as if he was worried that the slightest movement might disturb the flow of Sean Strong's story. "I followed him here to talk to him, tell him what he had done, and he just laughed it off. Said she had died because she was just an old carcass.

I grabbed him, and I shook him all right, Deputy. I would have liked to punch him in the face. But I didn't. I knew, even in that haze of anger, that there were better ways to get him. Take away his toys. His treasured possessions, his money, his budding television career, his good name. I left him alive, determined to hire the best lawyers in the business and strip him of everything he had. Bit by bit, so it would hurt the most."

Iphy patted his shoulder in silent sympathy.

Ace said, "When you left him, did you see anyone?"

"Just that assistant of his, the one who squealed about our argument and gave me away. No one else." Strong took a deep breath. "I was so angry I'm even surprised I could perform. But that is a lifetime's training. A routine."

"I'm very sorry about your mother's death." Ace sat up. "We need details about her and the objects missing from her home, so we can see if they're still among the dead man's possessions. Since you say that her lawyers knew what should have been there, there should be no problem proving these things belonged to her and returning them to the estate."

Strong sat with his head down. "It won't bring my mother back, Deputy."

"No," Ace said softly. "I can't do anything about that."

Callie caught his eye and saw the genuine compassion there and the anger at the criminal who had done this.

Strong said, "Now you know I had every reason to hate that man. But I didn't kill him." He looked up at Iphy. "I didn't."

"I know, Sean." Iphy smiled and put her hand against his face.

Callie stared at her great-aunt, the change that had come over her as she stood there with the man she had loved and lost fifty years ago. Such a long time and still her feelings seemed to be alive, as fresh as they had once been.

Ace said, "I must ask you to go back to your cell. I have a lot of things to check up on, and this information, although it's enlightening, doesn't clear you."

"I know." Strong drew breath slowly. "I should have looked after her better. I was away too much."

Iphy squeezed his shoulder.

Ace said, "She might not have told you about this man anyway. Such conmen are very clever to attach themselves to people and drive a wedge between them and their family or friends so they don't confide in them."

"I let her down." Strong spoke as if he hadn't even heard Ace. "I should have been there for her, and I wasn't. She died. I will never forgive myself for that."

Iphy squeezed his shoulder again, but he got up abruptly and walked to the door. "I'll go back to my cell now, Deputy. I'm tired."

Ace got up and accompanied him.

Iphy stood staring at the closing door. She wrapped her arms around her shoulders and rubbed them as if she was suddenly cold.

Callie said, "He must feel better now that he's been able to tell the truth." Inside, though, she wondered if that was really so. Had it really made him feel better to put into words that he had let his mother down and she had died, the victim of a ruthless conman who had only cared for money, never for people?

"Yes, but Falk is right. It doesn't clear him. It gives him motive for the crime." Iphy paced up and down. "A huge motive even. Consider this: in the cases of those ladies, it was money and humiliation, a need to settle the score, even after years and years. But Sean's mother *died*. And recently. That makes him the ideal murderer. Full of vengeful thoughts when he came to Haywood Hall."

Iphy closed her eyes a moment. "Oh, everything I do just seems to make it worse." She snapped her eyes open again and added, "Also for you. I should never have involved you in it. It's my battle to fight, my past. I'm so sorry, Callie. Please forgive me."

Callie didn't really know what to say to that. She wanted to forgive Iphy as she did understand her mixed-up emotions, and she also felt sorry for Sean Strong and the predicament his mother's sad death had put him in.

But on the other hand, she felt the rift with Ace like a constant ache inside her and couldn't just say it didn't matter. It did.

Ace came back in. He shut the door and stood a moment, frowning hard, as if considering a difficult decision.

Iphy lowered her arms and said, "You have to go see that woman, Paula. She seems easier to handle. She's the one who lied about her aunt's inheritance. I bet she doesn't have an aunt at all. I mean, not an aunt who died and left her anything of value."

Ace raked through his hair. "I can't confront her over her lies about the aunt. I'm not supposed to know about them."

"Yet," Callie said. "You could go and interview her because of her card in the book. She'll tell you the same lies she told us initially, and then you can check on them and expose her. It will, in any case, widen the circle of people hurt by the dead expert's fraud, and that could help Strong's case."

Ace looked doubtful. "This Paula might be thinking up a new story as we speak." He tensed as he added, "Or be packing her bags."

"Then you have to hurry." Iphy made a gesture with both arms as if to shove him out the door.

Ace hesitated, grabbed his coat from the rack, and walked out.

Chapter Seventeen

Callie awoke with a feeling she hadn't slept all night. She recalled snippets of dreams in which she had been running up an endless staircase in Haywood Hall, carrying sheets with crucial information while the killer followed her, determined to take them away. Getting more and more exhausted while running, Callie had at some point stumbled, and the sheets had fallen from her hands, whirling around her like fall leaves, only not gold and red, but stark white.

Then they had turned into snow, and she had been out in an open field, in the cold, which had oddly not touched her at all. She had felt light and happy, knowing it was close to Christmas. In the distance, a sleigh pulled by black horses had approached, and as it closed in, she had seen Ace in it, an empty place beside him. She had been certain he was coming to pick her up and had watched excitedly as the sleigh drew near.

But the horses hadn't lessened their speed, and he had just breezed by, not even looking at her. The sleigh had passed her so closely, she had staggered backward and had fallen into the snow, which seeped into her clothes, into her very core, leaving her so dreadfully cold and alone.

Now awake, tossing and turning in her warm bed, Callie could still feel that cold. The cold of knowing Ace was angry with her, and last night hadn't made it better. She cringed again, thinking of the look on his face when he had heard they had contacted Delacorte again. That had been wrong of them, but what else could they have done? Iphy was dead set on clearing Strong, and Callie couldn't just let her emotional great-aunt struggle on her own.

She groaned and lay on her back, rubbing her face. A sound from beside the bed drew her attention, and little Daisy was sitting there, looking at her as if she sensed her human could do with some cuddles.

Callie sat on the edge of the bed and lifted the dog in her arms, enjoying the warmth of her body as she crept close against her, making soft sounds. "I still have you, girl," Callie whispered. "You don't understand what's been going on, but even if you knew, you wouldn't be angry at me—I know that. You're always there for me, and that's why I love you so much."

She sat for a few more minutes, just soaking up the dog's wordless support, and then she decided to go down and make herself a big breakfast. She put Daisy down, gave her a last pat, then went to shower and dress.

Twenty minutes later, Callie was setting the table and keeping an eye on the croissants she had popped in the oven to get warm. She was boiling eggs and pressing fresh juice and digging through the cupboard for walnuts to add to the yogurt. Honey too, maybe.

She jerked upright when she heard a noise at the back door. She checked her watch. Wasn't it a bit early for social calls?

Then she suddenly, optimistically, hoped it was Ace and ran for the door. But to her surprise, it was Paula.

Or the woman calling herself Paula.

She was dressed in a short red jacket, jeans, and ankle boots. She gave Callie a pleading look. "Hello there. Can I come in for a moment? I have something to discuss with you."

Callie wasn't sure she actually wanted to let this woman into her kitchen, her home.

Paula seemed to sense her doubts and said, "I won't stay long. I just need to tell you something. Please? It could be important."

Callie's curiosity won out over her reluctance, and she nodded and let the woman in. She took the pan with eggs from the stove and leaned against the sink, keeping a watchful eye on Paula, who pulled out a chair and sat down at the kitchen table.

Daisy sniffed around her ankle boots, but Paula seemed too preoccupied to notice or acknowledge her.

Paula launched into her story. "Last night your fiancé was at the hotel. The deputy. He found the card in the book and wanted to know if I knew the victim personally. Of course, it is a bit odd to invite someone to your hotel room like that."

Paula laughed nervously. "I think he even suspected me of being the type who seduces and robs elderly gentleman. He is quite formidable when he looks at you like that. He was writing down what I said, and I knew if he took me to the station, he would also be taping it."

She entwined her fingers. "I . . . uh . . . I got a bit nervous, so I told him everything. Sylvia will be livid when she finds out."

Paula wet her lips. "Actually, I want to leave before she finds out."

"But you can't. If you leave, it will look really suspicious." Callie felt she had to say something like that, to ensure the women stuck around Heart's Harbor for the time being.

Paula said, "I don't feel sorry for Sylvia. She can fend for herself. I'm sure if the deputy tried to get anything from her, she'd just laugh in his face and not say a word. But Jane—"

"Jane?" Callie asked. "Who's Jane?"

"Jane is the woman Sylvia met through the magazine article she read about victims of conmen. She told you, remember?"

Callie tilted her head. "I thought that was you. The way she told it, there's a third woman involved?"

"Yes. Jane." Paula rubbed her hands together. "Jane was the one who told her story in the magazine. The story that was almost identical to Sylvia's. They struck up a friendship and vowed to hunt down this man who had hurt them. Jane is a colleague of mine. She asked me to help them execute this plan."

"So you aren't a victim of Mr. King?" Callie asked, perplexed by this new information.

"Not directly, no. But when Jane was seeing him and lending him money, she didn't have access to much and borrowed from me. Of course when he left her and couldn't be found anymore, I also didn't get my money back." Paula smiled sadly. "When Sylvia told us she had found the perfect occasion to confront him, we thought we could pull it off. I was supposed to ask him for the meeting, since he had never seen me and . . . I was youngest and better looking. They said he preyed on pretty women, you know."

Or old and defenseless women, Callie thought, recalling Sean's mother and feeling anger shoot through her veins again.

Paula swallowed. "I just wanted to help them both with a little justified revenge. I had no idea that . . ."

She fidgeted with her watch band. "When it was time to leave for the event, I had my doubts about it, and Sylvia decided she'd go with me to ensure I wouldn't chicken out at the last minute." Paula cringed, as if recalling Sylvia's criticism of her on the occasion. "Jane didn't want to come. She said that she didn't have the nerve and was afraid King would somehow recognize her. Sylvia's looks have changed a lot since her time with King, you know—different hairstyle and color—but Jane is the type you'd still recognize, even if you went to high school with her and hadn't seen her since. We agreed it was better if she stayed at the hotel. But I think . . . I wonder . . ."

Paula looked up at Callie, her eyes wide and insecure.

"If Jane went to the event anyway, confronted King, and killed him?" Callie asked. Her heart raced with the possibility that there might be another suspect in play. A potential killer Ace knew nothing about. What if this could clear Sean Strong? Iphy would be so happy!

Paula said hurriedly, “I don’t think Jane is a killer. Honestly not. She’s a kind woman and wouldn’t hurt a fly. But this whole thing with that man—it changed her. She felt so humiliated, and her kids also laughed at her. That mom had fallen for a conman. She had to fess up to them, you know, when they found out she was in debt.”

Paula looked sad. “I loaned her money to prevent her from going into debt. But she was so in love with him that she kept giving him money. Even after I asked her whether it was really such a good idea.” Paula’s eyes were full of tears. “I just can’t stand people ruining other people’s lives. And just for money! Not even for—”

“Something substantial.” Callie nodded. “I understand what you mean. Do you have a specific reason for thinking Jane went to the event anyway? I mean, if you made the agreement she wouldn’t show herself there and everything went down according to plan . . .”

Paula took a deep breath. “I saw her. When the concert was about to begin, I came from the restrooms. I saw Jane running down the stairs. I’m sure it was her. I’ve worked with her for six years now. I know her posture and movements, you know.”

Callie nodded. “So Jane fled the scene, so to speak?”

“That’s what it felt like. I was surprised she had come. I wondered if she was looking for us, but the concert was about to begin, and when I came down I didn’t see her anymore. There were so many people milling about. So I went back to Sylvia. I did tell her I thought I had seen Jane, but Sylvia said it must have been someone that looked like her. When you came to the hotel to talk to us, I wondered if I should mention Jane, but Sylvia signaled me not to."

Callie recalled that moment when Paula had asked Sylvia 'Should I . . .?' and before she had been able to end her sentence, Sylvia had shaken her head and launched into her story about how she had been conned by King. Paula had wanted to call in Jane, and Sylvia had prevented it.

Did Sylvia know Jane had been there and had perhaps killed the expert? Was she covering for her?

But why?

Or had the two women agreed on the murder together and only used Paula as a decoy?

Callie leaned against the sink. "So you didn't tell Ace—I mean, Deputy Falk—anything about Jane?"

"No. Just about Sylvia. I was worried that if he went to Jane, with his stern look and his gleaming badge and his notebook, she'd feel intimidated and might say something silly, incriminating herself. I don't think she killed King. Honestly."

Then why are you here? Callie asked her in silence.

It did seem that Paula wanted her, and via her the police, to know that Jane was a part of it.

Why?

Because Paula realized that she was in trouble, with her name on the card left in the book, her lies about her aunt's inheritance? Did she want to make sure she wouldn't be left holding the bag while Sylvia and Jane walked away unscathed?

That made total sense. But it was also possible that Paula was the killer and now wanted to shift the blame to Jane. After all, Paula was the only one declaring Jane had actually been at the event, that she had seen her there. That could be a lie.

And by revealing that she, Paula, had only been remotely involved in the conman's actions, not a direct victim, she underlined that she had no pressing reason to kill him. Sylvia and Jane did, right? Jane maybe most of all, as she had ended up in debt and embarrassed.

Callie sighed. "Now what do you want me to do?"

"Tell your fiancé what I told you. I won't make a statement against Jane. Not like that. She's my colleague. But he can look into her presence on the scene, right? Maybe take her fingerprints or something and see if they were anywhere near the victim? Somehow get hard proof. If there is none, it would clear her."

"Deputy Falk does need a reason to do that." Callie studied Paula. "Maybe he can just tell Jane that he interviewed you as part of the proceedings and asked who you were here with, in Heart's Harbor, in which case you would have had to mention both Sylvia and Jane."

Paula's expression brightened. "That's perfect! Her full name is Jane Williams, and she's in room 402." She rose to her feet. Now she noticed Daisy and crouched to pat her. "Nice doggy. Hello. Yes, you're very pretty. And soft."

Daisy closed her eyes as the woman scratched her behind the ears. The dog was usually a good judge of character, but

Callie didn't think she could now simply deduce that Paula was innocent in King's murder.

Maybe the three women had done it together, assuming that the police could never attribute the blame to one of them distinctly enough to press charges. Who had held the scissors stabbing the man to death?

Paula straightened up. "I told you all I know. Do with it what you think is right. I have to run along now, or Sylvia will miss me at breakfast. She is quite a force. Goodbye." She walked out of the door.

Callie stood considering. Yes, Sylvia was quite a force, but Paula seemed to have her ways as well. Quiet, soft-spoken, just a little insecure. But planting the seeds of doubt with great ingenuity. Jane, so humiliated, Jane present at the event. Sylvia wanting to protect Jane, and what for? Unless, of course, there was something Jane had done that had better not come to light.

It was well played.

Deliberately, to keep Paula from the spotlight?

Callie pursed her lips, staring at the table. She didn't feel like eggs and yogurt with walnuts and honey anymore. Her stomach seemed too full to eat anything. Full of murder and manipulation, with no clear clues leading her anywhere.

Chapter Eighteen

Having drunk a cup of coffee and eaten half a banana, Callie put the other half in her pocket and took Daisy to the Book Tea. They found Iphy busy putting some fresh white chocolate strawberry cookies on a plate she covered with plastic wrap.

Callie told her all about the third woman, Jane, while Iphy whipped cream to put in the fridge and use later on treats.

Concluding, Callie remarked, "I think it's a bit convenient to just assume Jane did it. Paula may claim to have seen her at the event, but we only have Paula's word for it. She could be lying to divert attention from herself. After all, I'm sure she's not happy Ace came after her at the hotel. Whether she believes he was just following up on the card in the book or not."

Iphy didn't respond. She seemed to be deep in thought. Callie poked her gently, and Iphy jerked upright and stared at her. "What?"

"Do you think Jane did it? Killed Mr. King?"

Iphy shook her head. "I think we've been misled all along."

"Misled?" Callie queried. "How do you mean?"

Iphy pointed at her, color rising in her cheeks. "I've been thinking all night long about what Sean told us, about his mother. There was something in his story that I was sure was connected to something we heard before."

"Yes, that the expert preyed on people for money."

"No, I mean something more specific. A clue, as it were." Iphy grinned. "And now I know what it is."

Her expression sobered as she added, "Not that it makes me happy to suspect him. If I'm right . . ." She tutted and shook her head. "Poor young man."

"Who are you talking about?"

"Seth Delacorte, of course. Remember how Mrs. Forrester told us that the expert yelled at him and treated him in a demeaning way?"

Callie tilted her head. "Is that a motive for murder? It seems to me Delacorte isn't the type to bark back, let alone defend himself with physical violence." She could still see him with his tousled hair and his pajamas, his bare feet, sitting on the edge of his bed, pulling up his legs and hugging his knees like a lost little boy in boarding school.

Iphy shook her head. "It's not the bullying behavior per se. I finally remembered what I had been trying to remember all night long. You see, Sean told us he was so upset about his mother being duped because she died. He believes that her bad experience influenced her health to that extent that it caused her death. So he could feel like the expert murdered his mother, indirectly."

"Yes, but what does that have to do with Delacorte?"

"He told us his father lost his job and could no longer pay for his tuition. And later he said his father had died."

"Yes, so?" Callie still didn't follow along.

"Well, maybe his father was a victim of King's machinations, and he lost his job because of that. Then he died. Delacorte might have wanted revenge for that."

Although Callie couldn't totally exclude this possibility, it did strike her as highly unlikely. "Delacorte told us he came to work for King four years ago. Would he have waited for four years to get that revenge he was after? And wouldn't he have taken a risk that King would find out he was related to one of his earlier victims?"

Iphy waved off her questions. "I think it's a viable theory. Sylvia said the assistant followed him around like a puppy. And Sean saw no one when he left the victim alone but that same assistant. So Delacorte might have gone in to King after the argument with Sean, where he grabbed and shook King after he maligned his mother. Maybe Delacorte even overheard part of what was said. The derogatory reference to an old woman as a carcass. He realized that his boss hadn't just ruined his father's life, but that of others as well. Maybe Sean's tale made Delacorte's anger over his father well up fresh, and he grabbed the scissors and stabbed his boss."

Callie wasn't sure that this scenario fit with Delacorte's character. But then how well did she really know him?

Maybe he had played the part of the shocked and insecure assistant although he did know more about it.

Something niggled at the back of her brain, something she had noticed when they had first visited Delacorte at the Cliff Hotel, but she couldn't lay her finger on what it was.

"I'll call Ace to tell him about Jane," she said to Iphy, "and then I can also ask him to look into Delacorte and see if he can find out more about how his father died and how he lost his job—if there could have been a relation with King's fraudulent activities."

Iphy nodded. "I hope Falk finds out something soon. I can't bear to think of Sean locked up." She shivered and then returned to work, finalizing preparations for Book Tea to open soon.

Callie called Ace and explained what she had learned. He said he was taking note of it, but she had the impression he was a bit distracted as he hemmed and hawed quite a few times and didn't reply when she had finished speaking. She had to ask twice if he had followed along, before he said, "Sure. Talk to you later," and disconnected.

Callie stared at the phone, then shrugged and put it back in her purse. Daisy had come to sit at her feet and was looking up at her expectantly.

With the same eagerness, Iphy asked if Falk was taking action right away.

"I don't know—he sounded kind of wrapped up. I assume he also has other cases on his hands."

Iphy seemed to want to say something, but then she just nodded and set up some trays with empty cups, ready to start pouring coffee and tea the moment the first customers came in.

Callie went into the tearoom and walked past all the tables, checking that the cloths were clean and there were no dead flowers on the plants. She was on her knees, peeling off the carpet a bit of bubblegum that the vacuum cleaner had apparently missed, as the door opened behind her, and Peggy came in. She looked better than she had in days, wearing a crisp white blouse and a knee-length skirt and high heels. Daisy ran for her and circled her while she came over to Callie. Peggy said, "I'm so sorry I didn't call you about this last night, but I can't work this morning. I have to drive into another town. For . . ."

She waited a moment as if undecided, then added, ". . . a job interview."

Callie's jaw sagged. "I thought you were happy here at Book Tea."

"Yes, but it's so close to the community center, and I feel awkward running into Quinn all the time. I think we . . . uh . . . need a bit of time away from each other."

Callie wanted to say something, but Peggy put a hand on her arm. "*I* need a bit of time away from it all. I'm not sure how I feel about Quinn. I do like him an awful lot—he's been a great friend, also to the boys, and I don't want to just say no. Just because he's a friend, I need to find out how I really feel. Whether I could . . . you know."

"Fall in love with him?" Callie asked softly.

Peggy nodded. "I'm so confused now. I feel guilty about Greg, and I'm comparing Quinn to Greg, and what I feel for

Quinn compared to what I felt when I met Greg, and it's just a mess. I have to give myself some space."

"Is it a nice job you're applying for?" Callie asked.

"Shop assistant in a ladies' boutique." Peggy gestured to her outfit. "Do you think I look the part?"

"Very crisp and professional," Callie assured her. "And you have good taste in clothes."

"But no retail experience, unless you count the three weeks I worked in a store when I was sixteen." Peggy grimaced. "I just hope they'll give me a chance." She leaned over and added hurriedly, "I do hope you won't think I'm ungrateful, Callie. I loved working here, and if Quinn hadn't suddenly said all those things, I would never have walked out on you like this. But right now . . ."

"I totally understand. I hope you get the job and can have that time away to make up your mind. Quinn wouldn't be happy either if you just threw yourself into a relationship with him without having considered it first. I'm sure he'll understand."

Peggy nodded and checked her watch. "I have to run. Thanks so much. Now I don't feel so bad about leaving you." She looked down and seemed to notice Daisy, squatting to give her a scratch behind the ears. The dog tilted her head and barked as if wishing her good luck.

Peggy straightened and rushed to the door, then halted, her hand on the handle. "Oh, I told Ace what happened. I didn't want him to blame you for anything."

Callie wanted to ask how Ace had taken this, but Peggy was already out the door. Daisy, who had followed her, ambled back to Callie and sniffed the last bit of bubblegum left on the spot Callie had been cleaning.

Callie released her breath in a huff. Losing Peggy meant losing very good help in the Book Tea. Which meant more work for them.

She got back on her knees to finish cleaning.

* * *

During lunchtime, having served countless people the daily special, Callie was clearing an outside table when she spied Ace on the other side of the street, talking to a colleague who was giving parking tickets.

Just as Callie turned to carry the dirty cups and plates inside, she almost collided with Iphy, who came jogging out and headed straight for Ace, paying so little attention to the traffic in the street that a small truck honked at her.

Ace turned his head at the honk and saw Iphy coming for him. Judging by his expression as he leaned over to her once she was there, he reprimanded her about her careless way of crossing the street, but Iphy didn't seem to give him a chance to finish, putting her hand on his arm. Ace led her away from his colleague, who continued to check cars that might not belong there.

Callie couldn't resist watching how her great-aunt, a frail figure compared to tall, broad Ace, pleaded with him while he shook his head and seemed to want to calm her down. The sun reflected off his badge as he moved to speak to her with even more emphasis.

At last, Iphy turned in a jerk and ran back across the street, again barely watching where she went. A blue sedan braked and honked, and Ace stood there shaking his head. He spotted Callie and seemed to want to come over to her, but then he reached into his pocket, pulled out his phone, and took a call. He listened intently, said something, and rushed off to his car, which was parked nearby.

Callie shrugged and carried her tray of dirty dishes inside. Iphy was in the kitchen, filling a three-tiered stand for a tea party coming in at two thirty. She clanked the bonbons onto the china so hard that the toppings almost came off.

Callie caught her arm. "What?"

"Falk just doesn't want to listen to me. I'm sure Delacorte knows more than he's telling us, and I have the perfect plan to find out just what he knows."

"I'm sure Ace went after the leads we gave him. In fact, I saw that he got a call just now and rushed off. He must be getting on with the case." Callie didn't know what the call had been about, of course, but her great-aunt was so worked up, she'd say anything to calm her down a bit. She gently ushered Iphy out of the way and finished dressing the stand for her.

Iphy stood there, breathing hard, and then said, "Oh, well, if nobody wants to listen," and stomped out of the kitchen. Footfalls on the stairs suggested she was rushing up to her bedroom. Daisy ran after her, barking as if telling her to stop and wait for her.

Callie shook her head. Her great-aunt would calm down again, she hoped, and see reason. After all, Ace was doing the best he could. He just had a lot on his plate with the sheriff being indisposed and all.

She heard the floor creak upstairs and raised her head a moment to listen as the footfalls stopped. Had Iphy sat down or maybe even lain down on her bed? Daisy could give her some cuddles and cheer her up. Maybe Iphy even wanted to have a little nap, to gather energy before facing her tea party guests.

Callie nodded to herself. An excellent idea. She hoped Iphy would fall into a deep, dreamless sleep that would reinvigorate her. If Iphy didn't come down before two thirty, Callie would receive the tea party and serve them with the other helpers. Iphy needed a bit of a break to regain her usual cool. Over dinner they might have a talk and see if there was any more they could do for Sean Strong.

* * *

Just after six, Callie closed up Book Tea and stood, stretching her stiff shoulders. The afternoon had passed in a rush of people coming and going. Especially five ladies dropping in unannounced to have a high tea, which had been a bit of a hassle, but Callie had made everything work out, sending a helper across the street to the general store for fresh raspberries to work into an impromptu trifle topped off with crumbled meringue. The women had laden her with compliments and assured her they'd recommend the tearoom to all of their friends, so Callie had been quite happy with how it had turned out.

Nevertheless, she was exhausted now and eager for some hot food. But first she would go see her great-aunt, who she assumed was still in bed, with Daisy watching over her.

Callie was glad, on the one hand, that Iphy had fallen asleep and was getting some much-needed rest, but on the other hand, it did worry her that she would truly be so exhausted that she had simply slept away the entire afternoon.

Callie tiptoed up the stairs and listened at her great-aunt's bedroom door. No sound. She knocked softly and opened the door a crack. "How are you? Want some dinner? I can make pizza, if you like. Maybe some fresh juice to go with it?"

No reply.

Callie opened the door wider and looked in. The bed was messy, as if someone had indeed lain down on it, but her great-aunt was nowhere to be seen. Daisy came for Callie, jumping against her and wagging her tail. Callie scooped the dog into her arms and looked about her as if she expected Iphy to materialize. No one.

Then her eye fell on a note left on the dressing table. She rushed over and picked it up. It read, "I will be back soon. Don't worry. I know what I'm doing."

That exact wording got Callie worried. Very worried.

What had Iphy been up to when she had snuck away? Why had she not simply said where she was going and what she had in mind?

Callie studied the note with a frown, the images coming back to her of Iphy's encounter with Ace in the street. What had she discussed with him? Obviously, he hadn't wanted to agree, whatever it was. Had Iphy then decided to take action on her own? Had she only pretended to go to bed to rest? How long had she been gone anyway?

With Daisy in her arms, Callie ran back downstairs. In the kitchen, she picked up her phone and called Ace. It rang and rang without answer, then went to voicemail, and she told him to call her back first thing as it was urgent.

She paced the room, Daisy hard on her heels, waiting for him to call, but nothing happened. She tried his number again. Voicemail. Another message.

Who cared if he thought she was pushy? This was Iphy they were talking about. Iphy, who seemed to be missing.

Iphy, who could be . . . in danger?

Nonsense, Callie tried to tell herself. Iphy had probably asked Ace for information he wasn't allowed to give out, and then she decided to go and hire a PI or something. Or talk to Sean Strong's lawyer. Or some other perfectly normal thing. It didn't mean she was doing something risky.

But Callie couldn't forget how her normally careful great-aunt had almost caused a collision—twice!—rushing across the street without watching where she was going. To catch Ace. Who had not wanted to help her. What if she had then decided she needed to act on her own? After all, she had felt so sorry about involving Callie earlier. At the police station, after seeing Sean Strong, she had even asked Callie for forgiveness for dragging her into it. Had she then decided to continue sleuthing by herself?

Her phone rang, and Callie almost dropped it. She answered, "Yes?" in a hoarse voice.

"What is so urgent?" Ace sounded irritated. "I was in an interrogation, and the other deputy told me my phone kept ringing. I thought it might be something to do with Peggy or the boys."

"Peggy is fine. I thought she talked to you."

"Yes, she's now thinking of taking a job away from town, all because of that guy Quinn. I wish they had never met."

"She's just changing jobs, not moving away." Callie felt obliged to stem his annoyance. "And Quinn genuinely cares for her. I'm hoping Peggy will come to see that." Maybe once she got settled in her new job, she would find out she missed Quinn and their regular lunches, and they'd get together anyway.

Callie took a deep breath as she realized this wasn't what Ace wanted to hear right now or what she herself needed to know from him. With a vague hope that Jane Williams could be the killer and Ace had her at the station so she'd pose no danger to Iphy, she asked, "Did you get a chance to speak to Jane Williams and ask her about her presence at the event?"

"Yes, she admitted she went there to look for her friends and dissuade them from confronting King. But she claims she never saw King himself. I'm checking with a few people who gave fairly detailed witness statements about happenings shortly before King died, to see if they remember seeing a woman of Jane Williams's physical description around. But I doubt it will turn up much."

Callie's uneasy feeling intensified. If Ace was right about Jane, the killer was still lurking in the shadows. "What did Iphy discuss with you this afternoon."

"Didn't she tell you? Sulking because I didn't agree?" Ace sounded grim. "I'm not risking her safety in some stupid confrontation that won't bring anything I can work with."

"Confrontation?" Callie echoed. Her heart rate sped up, and she supported herself on the back of a chair. Daisy pressed herself against her leg.

Ace sighed. "Iphy is convinced that the victim's assistant, this Seth Delacorte, knows more than he's let on. She wanted to set up a meeting between her and him where she'd get him talking and I'd overhear everything and then arrest him or something. I told her that if he *is* the killer, he'll be too smart to let something slip. She wasn't happy, but hey—I had her best interest in mind."

"Did you find out more about Delacorte's past?" Callie asked, almost breathless.

"Seems like he told the truth. His father got kicked out of a law firm he worked at, and Delacorte couldn't finish college and went to work for our victim. His father then died. Of a heart attack—nothing incriminating. No connection with our victim either, at least none I can establish right away. There's no way of knowing, of course, if he duped Delacorte's father if the father never filed charges with the police or left evidence of it."

Callie's mind whirled. "If he left some evidence of it, among his private papers, it would have fallen into Delacorte's hands after his father died. When was that?"

"Eight months ago."

"Might that have made him decide that he would kill his boss?"

Ace scoffed. "He just happened to start working for the man who then later turned out to have ripped off his father? That would be a gigantic coincidence. I don't believe it for a moment."

It did seem extremely coincidental. But if Delacorte had known about the fraud from the start, why had he waited so long to take revenge?

And if he had only found out eight months ago, how could he have been working for the man who caused his father's misery without knowing that himself?

It didn't make sense either way.

Ace said, "Just leave the investigation to me, Callie. And keep an eye on Iphy. She seemed very excitable, and that kind of mood doesn't lead to smart decisions."

"That's why I am calling you." Callie swallowed before she could go on. "She isn't here. She left a note telling me not to worry, that she'd be okay."

"What?" Ace sounded like he had shot upright in his chair on hearing this news. "She's not with you at Book Tea?"

"No. And I have no idea how long ago she left here."

Ace muttered something under his breath. "Do you know where she went? What she intends to do?"

"No, she didn't tell me anything—not even what she discussed with you. She was so upset about not getting the help she obviously wanted that she went straight upstairs, and I figured she'd just had it and needed a rest, so I left her alone. I just now found the note, and I'm worried she believed she couldn't ask me for help as it had only gotten me into trouble before. I did feel bad about the way we kept things from you, and Iphy was really sorry about her actions. But she feels like she can't let Strong down either."

Ace sighed. "I don't think she would do something, really. She does realize she would be—could be facing—"

Callie clutched the phone. "Now you suddenly suspect Delacorte?"

"Not at all, but you never know what people will do when they feel cornered. Private citizens should not go after . . . well, people they suspect of being involved in crimes."

"They might feel like they have to when the police are doing nothing."

"You agree with her?"

"No, but I did observe how you turned her away this afternoon. She didn't feel like you were taking her seriously." Callie bit her lip. "You also didn't tell me to keep an eye on her." She felt terribly guilty now for having left Iphy to herself in the emotional state she had been in.

"I got a call about a burglary in progress. I couldn't just ignore that." Ace's voice was sharp. Then he said, "Look, Callie, we can't argue now about who's to blame here. We have to find out where she went."

Yes, of course. Callie pushed a hand against her face. Her cheek seemed hot, her hand super cold, and she shivered. "What did she tell you exactly? Did she mention a place for this meeting with Delacorte where she would provoke him into revealing something?"

"No, I don't think so." Ace sounded doubtful. "I told her right away I didn't want to do it, so when she started explaining the details to me, I wasn't really listening all that well anymore. I mean, come on—this has to stop somewhere."

Callie closed her eyes. "Where would she think was a good meeting place?"

"At the hotel? That would be safest, with other people around."

Callie tried to focus, but fear churned in her stomach. Why hadn't she realized just how much Sean Strong meant to Iphy? How the reunion with him had brought back all the memories of falling in love with him in the first place but also of letting him down, choosing the safer option, not wanting to take risks. Iphy was a determined person who wanted to do the right thing. She had judged her earlier actions as those of a coward and obviously felt the need to prove she wasn't afraid anymore.

Clenching her free hand into a fist, Callie took a deep breath. Her great-aunt's behavior had confused and frustrated her, but right now she only knew one thing for certain. She should have offered to help her. Then they might now both be in danger, but that would have been better than her great-aunt trying to do this alone. It could only end in disaster.

In death even?

Callie swallowed hard. *Focus! The hotel as a meeting place? Can that be it?*

She narrowed her eyes as she zoomed in on details that had previously been just out of her grasp. Delacorte's hotel room, the bed with the duvet folded away but the sheet covering the mattress undisturbed, the scent in the room and the condensation on the table.

"He didn't get out of bed when we came to his door," she said slowly. "He was up and about. He had sat there drinking. The scent I noticed—sweetness—it was of liquor. He had put the glass away, out of sight, after the receptionist called him and told him that we were coming up to his room. The ring on the table gave away that a glass had stood there. He wasn't groggy from sleeping off the sedative—that was just an act. He was sitting there, drinking, maybe even toasting himself on his success."

"What?" Ace asked.

Callie's thoughts were racing. "And at our second meeting, over dinner, he cleverly drew our attention to Paula and Sylvia. His smile when we left the table in a rush to go after those two women wasn't a knowing little smile, realizing our curiosity, but a satisfied smile that his plan was working. To divert attention, make others look suspicious."

She could just kick herself that she hadn't noticed sooner. But she had sympathized with Delacorte's position, had felt sorry for the nice, unobtrusive young man who was bullied by his boss. Even now she wasn't sure they were on the right track. It was so hard to believe that they would have dined with the killer, even thinking that if the murder hadn't happened, it could have been a pleasant night!

"Look." Ace's voice sounded softer. "I do recall Iphy said something about a vase. Payment, she called it. It didn't make sense to me, but she said it."

"A vase? Payment?" Callie snapped her eyes open. "That must be the vase Mrs. Forrester mentioned to us, the one the dead expert had asked for. A vase from the collection at Haywood Hall."

"Okay. So we could go to Haywood Hall and see if she's there."

"We?"

Ace laughed softly. "I have no illusions I can keep you out of this, Callie. Not with Iphy's safety at stake. Better to have you with me where I can keep an eye on you."

Callie felt a bit annoyed that he expected her to get into trouble, but she had to acknowledge that the panic inside could be coloring her judgment. For Iphy she'd do anything. Blindly.

"I'll grab my coat and take Daisy to a neighbor. Pick me up as fast as you can."

Chapter Nineteen

They arrived at Haywood Hall and left the police car a bit away from the house as Ace explained to Callie it might be better not to draw attention. "If Delacorte is here for some reason, I don't want him spooked."

They continued on foot, approaching the house as if they were a couple of burglars attempting a break in. Around back they came to the door into the kitchen area and found Mrs. Keats there, making sandwiches. Callie knocked on the window, and the surprised housekeeper dropped the cheese and ham to let them in.

Callie smiled at her, determined not to create panic in this usually quiet household. "Hello—sorry for barging in like this, but did you see Iphy this afternoon?"

"Yes, she was here earlier. She needed to look into some books, so she went upstairs. I don't know if she's still here."

Callie looked at Ace, her emotions swaying between relief and disbelief. Books? Just books? Had her great-aunt believed there was a clue in there somewhere?

Ace said to Mrs. Keats, "Do you mind if we go see her for a moment? It's urgent."

"Oh. Not at all. I'm making sandwiches for the evening meal. Do you want to eat with us?"

"Maybe." Ace smiled at her, but Callie noticed the tension in his posture. He wanted up, up, up to find Iphy. And so did she.

They left the kitchen and walked through the hallway, up the broad stairs. Callie clung to the railing. If they found her great-aunt there, innocently leafing through books, she'd be so relieved; she felt she could almost shake her and shout at her. But she would tell her later how she had felt.

Ace opened the door into the library. No one there. Callie felt her hopeful feeling dissipating. Her heart beat fast again, and she just couldn't bear the tension building.

Ace tried the nearby study. No one there.

He looked at her. "She made up an excuse to gain access to the house and find the vase she needed for her meeting with Delacorte. The so-called payment. Which one is it?" He looked about him at the several antiquities on display.

Callie shrugged. "I don't know. Mrs. Forrester never told us. Besides, Iphy wouldn't lie her way in here to take a vase that doesn't belong to her."

"She must have told herself she would be returning it later."

Callie shook her head in disbelief. But Ace caught her arm. His eyes were insistent, pleading. "Strong told me that once upon a time he loved Iphy, and he believed she loved him. People do the oddest things for love. What do you know about the vase, Callie?"

"Nothing. Mrs. Forrester didn't mention a brand or how old it was, what it looked like. I can't point out where it should be either, to check if it's still there. Sorry."

Ace let go of her and took a deep breath. Then he said, "Check all the rooms to see if she's there. If not . . ."

They each ran in a direction, throwing open doors and looking in. Callie's heart was thumping. She wanted to find Iphy, no matter what. But she didn't see anyone.

Ace came up to her, defeat in his features. "She's not here. What now?"

"What did she tell you about this meeting she wanted to set up with Delacorte? Aside from the vase?"

Ace lifted both hands in a helpless gesture. "I told you I wasn't really listening. I had told her I was not okay with it, and it just annoyed me how she kept going on about it."

Callie stood in front of him, holding his gaze. "Try to recall something—anything. Please."

Ace closed his eyes a moment, as if to focus completely on recalling those moments in the sunny street with Iphy beside him, explaining her plan. He shook his head with an irritated sigh. "She only mentioned the vase and some quiet spot for the meeting."

"Quiet spot? Around here?"

Ace thought again. "Yes, I think so. She said something about the vase being precious and her not wanting it to leave the grounds."

Callie sucked in air. "Not leave the grounds? Then Iphy must be on the grounds belonging to Haywood Hall. We'll find her outside."

She ran off, Ace following her. As they raced down the stairs, he asked, "Do you think she called Delacorte for a meeting? Did she have his phone number?"

Callie nodded. "He gave me a card with his contact information. She could have taken it out of my purse."

Ace looked grim. "I should have known about all of this. Then I . . ." They were in the hallway and ran out the front door, closing it behind them. They looked outside, around the house, peeking into windows and the conservatory. But they didn't spot a sign of life.

Callie stood, gasping for breath.

Ace looked about him. "Maybe away from the house?"

Callie jerked upright. "That's it! The old stables. They're no longer in use—they just sit empty. They're large and—"

Ace cut her off with a brisk movement and gestured for her to come along. His hand was on his weapon, but he didn't draw it yet.

Callie followed him, with the blood pounding in her ears. What had Iphy gotten herself into?

At the stables, Callie showed Ace the narrow side door. The padlock on it was open. Ace nodded at it, and Callie nodded in return to acknowledge she had seen it and understood what it meant. They could no longer speak now because of the risk of being overheard. Someone was inside.

Ace pushed the door open slowly. It didn't creak. Inside it was dim. Callie had to blink a few moments before she started to discern things. The old stalls for the horses, some gear against the walls, and there in the center . . . Iphy, with a vase cradled in her arms. Delacorte standing opposite her.

Callie froze and stared at her great-aunt, so brave and so foolish. Her first impulse was to call out to her so that Delacorte would know they were not alone and wouldn't do anything sudden. Assuming he had something to hide. But she kept quiet, listening to him speak. "Why offer the vase to me?" he said. "My boss was the one taking things where he could get them. I wanted no part in his actions."

"I know." Iphy sounded kind and compassionate. "I know everything. Your father first lost his job, his career, all he had built, and then also his life. Because of this wicked man who preyed on people. You went to work for him to confront him somehow, maybe get money back? I don't know what you intended, but I'm sure it wasn't murder. You killed him on impulse, maybe even self-defense. We can help you with the court case. I want to help you because I understand how you must have felt. Maybe he taunted you, said it didn't matter?"

Delacorte stood motionless, watching her. "I didn't harm him."

For a moment, Callie felt some tension slip away from her. Of course Delacorte wasn't the killer. Iphy had just pieced some information together and jumped to a conclusion. Delacorte would convince her it hadn't been him, and then, aside from some embarrassment over the rash accusation, no harm would have been done.

"It must have been you," Iphy said. "You overheard Mr. King's argument with Sean Strong. Mr. King laughed about the agony of his victims and even called Mr. Strong's mother an old carcass. Your anger about the injustice done to your father flared again, and you couldn't walk away. After

Mr. Strong left the room, you confronted King. Then it happened."

Iphy took a deep breath. "All I want is for you to admit you killed him. We'll hire the best lawyers to help you with your defense. Sean can testify what King did to his mother and how terribly he spoke about her. A jury will understand you acted in a moment of great emotional distress. Please don't let an old man go to prison for what you did. Sean's like your father. Think of him."

"He is nothing like my father." Delacorte sounded half amused. "Dear lady, you misunderstand completely." He stepped closer to her. "My father was fired from the law firm where he worked because he had done favors for clients. He liked fast money, you know. One of the clients was our Mr. King. I realized that he could be important to me. So I left college and started to work for him. Or should I say, he started to work for me?"

Iphy stared at Delacorte, her mouth half open.

Delacorte said, "You see, like my father, I love money. And King had connections he could use. He also never had scruples, so it wasn't hard to convince him to help me get my hands on pieces like that." He nodded at the vase.

Iphy said, "You asked for this?"

"Through him, yes. Via my father's network, I got in touch with people who deal in antiques. Do you know how much money collectors are prepared to pay for certain pieces? They don't ask where they come from either."

Callie stood motionless. The black market for antiquities and art. Of course.

Delacorte said, "The only problem was that King had been a bad little crook in the past. You know, swindling women for money. Small fries. He still couldn't stop conning people. Offering too little money for the books, grinning to himself like he was so smart. I told him to stop doing it, to focus on our big antiques scores. But no, he wouldn't listen. He also took on the TV engagement without consulting me first. I could have told him that it wasn't smart to have your face plastered across TV screens nationwide. But he was so vain he just couldn't say no. And as he was the front man of my operation, I couldn't just ditch him either. I just had to keep my fingers crossed that if trouble came our way, I could solve it, buy off the claimants or something. But here at the event, it wasn't a little old lady with a sad story. It was a well-known baritone who was angry enough to cause us serious trouble. I overheard part of the conversation all right. I realized where we were at. Everything we had worked for was at stake. If King came under investigation, it could also endanger me and my connections. They aren't the kind of people who appreciate police scrutiny, you understand? Yes, I think you do, but King didn't. When I confronted him, after that baritone had stormed off in a rage, King laughed it off, and he even mentioned to me some Paula who had left a card in a book for him, inviting him to her hotel room. He said he would go too. Because she was quite a dish—excuse the language—and because he thought he could get money out of her to keep their fling a secret. I couldn't believe he dared to . . ." Delacorte's voice was husky with anger. "I could no longer allow him to jeopardize it all with his messy little cons on the side."

"But with his death, your scheme has ended," Iphy protested.

"On the contrary. I have the connections, and people know me as that shy little assistant. Don't you think I could have gotten into people's houses and into their collections? I already thought up a new plan to profit from it. A smart plan. Too bad it now seems to have gone awry."

He looked Iphy over. "You may understand that I'm not going to sign any kind of confession and throw myself at the mercy of a jury. I'm leaving. But not alone."

Fast like lightning, he grabbed Iphy and pressed her against a support beam. He produced a rope and began to tie her hands. "You will be a nice bargaining chip should the police come after me before I can cross the state line and get on a plane to Europe."

Callie looked at Ace. He glanced back at her and shook his head to indicate he wasn't going to interfere now.

Callie agreed that it was better to wait until Delacorte tried to move her bundled-up great-aunt out of the stables to his car. Where would it be parked?

Iphy cried out in pain as the rope was pulled tight around her wrists.

Delacorte said, "I'll leave you in the trunk of the car when I park it in the airport parking lot. If you're lucky, you can make so much noise someone walking past will notice and free you. If not . . ." He clucked his tongue. "They do say curiosity kills old biddies, don't they?"

Callie would have liked to run over and smack him, but she couldn't be sure he wasn't armed. He was so close to Iphy he could easily harm her as soon as he noticed they weren't alone. If only out of spite that his escape plan was ruined.

Ace had drawn his gun but seemed hesitant to take aim and call out. Callie realized that, on hearing a voice, Delacorte could use Iphy as a human shield. Her heart beat so fast she could barely draw breath.

Delacorte knelt down quickly to put a rope around Iphy's ankles. Iphy was still holding the vase in her arms, clutched against her. She looked down at him and in a flash she lifted her arms and smashed the vase down on Delacorte's head. It broke in an explosion of shattering bits.

Delacorte made a gasping sound and then sagged to the floor.

Ace ran up to Iphy and asked in a rush, "Are you okay?" while he also leaned down over Delacorte to pull his limp arms behind his back and handcuff him.

Iphy looked at Ace with wide eyes. "Deputy!"

She stared a moment, her mouth half open and then said, "Oh, if I had known you were here and could arrest him, I needn't have—that precious vase! What will Mrs. Finster say?"

Chapter Twenty

They sat around the table in Haywood Hall's dining room, with sandwiches and hot tea. Iphy had apologized a thousand times for breaking the vase, but Dorothea said it didn't matter as long as the murder was solved and the real killer caught and brought to justice. Mrs. Keats produced salve to rub on the rope burn on Iphy's wrists, and Callie hovered over her, bringing water and scolding her for taking ten years off Callie's life with her actions. "Don't you ever do something like that again."

Ace left with Delacorte, to lock him up and file charges against him. Callie was surprised he hadn't lectured her great-aunt about her behavior, but maybe that was still to come? First things first, right?

Suddenly the doorbell rang, and Mrs. Keats stood to open the door.

Dorothea said she had no idea who might call at this hour, but then there was a bustle already, and Sean Strong walked in. He came straight for Iphy and said, "What have you done? The deputy told me you single-handedly apprehended King's killer to ensure I was released."

He looked down on her and shook his head. "You shouldn't have done that."

Callie cringed as she imagined Strong going on to explain that he really didn't have any feelings for Iphy that warranted such action.

But surely he wouldn't say so in the presence of others?

Strong didn't say anything. He just leaned over and kissed Iphy full on the lips.

Her befuddled great-aunt sat blushing and then said, "What was that for?"

"That's what I should have done when I walked through the door the other day." Strong smiled at her. "You're coming to Vienna with me. No—no excuses. I want to show you that great city. You need some time away. There are too many murders here."

Callie was certain her great-aunt would say no, as she had Book Tea to consider, but to her surprise, Iphy rose to her feet and threw her arms around Strong. She hugged him and said against his shoulder, "I would love that! When are we leaving?"

"Tomorrow, first thing." Strong patted her head. "I'm going to spoil you. The best dinners, a show of the white horses. The Ferris wheel."

It was odd to see her great-aunt in the arms of a man like that, but somehow it was also right. Callie couldn't help smiling. Iphy looked so happy and in place.

"You better get packing," Strong said, "I know how much stuff you think you need to take with you."

Iphy let go of him and said, "Not so fast, Sean Strong. We are going to dinner right now to celebrate your release." She turned to Callie. "I'm sure you will run Book Tea very well while I'm away, Callie. I'm so happy I can now leave it in capable hands."

"How long will you be gone?" Callie asked, overtaken by the whole situation.

"Three weeks," Iphy said, while Strong said, "Three months." They looked at each other and burst out laughing. They hugged again, kissed, and then ran off, hand in hand.

Past Ace, who stood in the doorway. Callie saw a hint of amusement in his eyes but also something sad. He looked at her and gestured for her to come over.

Leaving the others in the dining room, Callie walked out to stand in the hallway. Iphy and Strong were gone already. Outside a car engine started.

Ace said, "She took an awful chance there, but it seems she got rewarded for it. Strong told me when I released him that he once asked Iphy to come with him and share his traveling life, but she said no because of her ties to Heart's Harbor, Book Tea, everything she loves about this place. He believed that she'd made the right decision, for her, and didn't want to contact her again, even though, through the years, he thought of her every now and then. Now, as Mr. King had lured him to Heart's Harbor, he felt like it was somehow meant to be."

Before Callie could speak, Ace continued, "I won't say anything about her behavior this afternoon to you, because

I know you didn't know about it and didn't agree with it either. I know you'd never allow her to put herself in danger, and I saw firsthand, when we were looking for her, how afraid for her you were."

He took a deep breath. "Just because you felt that way, you must now understand how I feel about you. Your involvement in all of these cases." He shook his head. "I can ask you to promise to stop sleuthing after today, but you won't. You can't—you're too kindhearted and perhaps also just too determined once your mind is made up about something. You also have Book Tea now to take care of all alone, and Peggy's gone too."

He looked away. "You may be right that it's good for her to have a job away from town. I don't always approve of her choices, but I do realize I have to let her be. Maybe it's best that I'm not watching her too closely. I'll just trust in her own ability to make the right choices, for her future and the boys. We all need a bit of space, I guess."

He leaned back. "People have been talking about me becoming sheriff and all, now that our old sheriff isn't doing well. They say I did a great job replacing him, but it's all going too fast for me. I'm fine with working as a deputy here, but becoming sheriff—so soon? I don't know if I really want that. I might just ask to be placed at another office for a bit. Have time away from Heart's Harbor, see new places, different ways of handling things. Just so I can make up my mind about it all."

Callie looked him over. She felt sorry for the tiredness in his features. "Are you sure?"

"Yes." He smiled sadly as he reached out his hand and cupped her cheek. "I can't go on like it's been the past few weeks. There's too much going on right now, and it's influencing my judgment. I can't see straight. I need time away, to think about my job here in Heart's Harbor and about us. How our relationship can work when you challenge me about my cases, and—well, you were right again. I had the wrong suspect locked up."

"It's not a competition," Callie said quickly, but Ace stopped her with a hand gesture. "That's not what I mean."

He frowned as if looking for the right words. "I arrested Strong based on evidence, so I don't regret that choice. But Iphy showing up to plead for him rubbed me the wrong way. Not just because it was a civilian butting in on a case, but because of you. I wanted to know whose side you were on really, Iphy's or mine, and I started to make decisions based on emotion."

Ace swallowed hard. "Because I didn't listen to her carefully, Iphy could have been killed. You would never have forgiven me. I would never have forgiven myself. I feel like I can't be a good deputy this way, or a good partner for you. I have to think things over, figure out how I can make all of this work."

Callie's heart ached for him. "I do respect your judgment and your expertise on the cases. But Iphy is my closest family here and—"

"Shh." Ace caressed her cheek. "I understand. And because I understand, I have to do this. I have to go away, take time to think it over and make sure where I am at before

I . . ." He looked into her eyes, searching, it seemed. "I had planned for Valentine's Day to be completely different."

Callie's heart skipped a beat, thinking he might have had a special date in mind, with a special present. Would she ever find out what it was?

"At least Iphy is happy," Ace said. "I couldn't believe the change that came over her when Strong asked her to come with him."

"She's just accepting an old invitation. Fifty years after the fact." Callie had to smile despite her personal dejection about facing a separation from Ace, even if it was temporary. Iphy was indeed very happy now, also because in her absence her beloved Book Tea would continue to flourish in the hands of family. Even Grandfather Achilles would have approved of that. It made Callie warm inside and also confident that her bond with Ace could stand the test of being apart. They had something very special.

"Yes, well, I still have a lot to do," Ace said. "To ensure Delacorte will pay for what he did. Not just the murder but also the whole fraudulent scheme with antiques for the black market he was the mastermind of. I still can't grasp how a quiet type like him could be the real crook."

"Maybe just the bigger crook," Callie corrected. "King wasn't exactly innocent either. Think of the poor women he duped all those years ago."

Ace nodded. "I will contact them again, and we can see if something can be repaid to them. This will be a very big and complicated thing, so"—he rubbed his face—"I better get on it."

"Sure. And thanks for coming to save Iphy."

A smile lit his features. "I wouldn't have done anything less. She is one of the citizens I vowed to protect."

Yes. If Delacorte had been armed, Ace might have risked his safety in a confrontation. He might have been injured, or worse. Callie's stomach tightened just thinking about that. He had such a dangerous profession. Did she really want to be with him, get closer, marry, and then end up like Peggy? Losing her husband as he tried to save a life he had vowed to safeguard?

She let him out the door and watched as he hurried down the steps in front of Haywood Hall and into his police car. He looked back at her and waved. She waved back, feeling a bit of a burn behind her eyes.

Iphy had once said no to Sean Strong because her family's opinion, her comfortable life, security, and a place to settle had been more important to her than following her heart. Now she had made a choice again, this time chasing her feelings, choosing happiness, maybe only temporarily, as she knew Sean Strong so little, really, after all the years that had passed. But she had made her choice and taken a chance for it.

Maybe Callie just wasn't ready to do that? Maybe she was just holding on to too many securities, wanting to know exactly what the future would bring before surrendering herself to feel how much Ace actually meant to her. Maybe he wasn't the only one who had some thinking to do about their relationship and how they could make it work.

Ace drove off to the station, but soon he'd be going to another post. It would be for a while, not forever. He'd be back, and she might know better then what she wanted and how he might fit in to that.

And however things turned out and whatever she decided, she'd still have Book Tea, the tea parties, Daisy, her new home. Her friendship with so many people who had also helped her with this case. And Haywood Hall, the place she had signed up to conserve and care for.

Callie smiled up at its majestic front before going back in to where the others were waiting with their sandwiches. Valentine's Day might not have turned out the way she had imagined it, but it had shown her she was part of a community where people cared for one another and braved the storms together. A community with a lot of heart.

Acknowledgments

As always, I'm grateful to all agents, editors, and authors who share online about the writing and publishing process. A special thanks to my amazing agent, Jill Marsal; my wonderful editor, Faith Black Ross; and the entire talented crew at Crooked Lane Books, especially cover illustrator Brandon Dorman for the heartwarming cover. And of course to you, reader: thanks for picking up this story and spending time in Heart's Harbor.